First Date

Books by Melody Carlson

Devotions for Real Life
Double Take
Just Another Girl
Anything but Normal
Never Been Kissed
Allison O'Brian on Her Own—Volume 1
Allison O'Brian on Her Own—Volume 2
A Simple Song

LIFE AT KINGSTON HIGH
The Jerk Magnet
The Best Friend
The Prom Queen

the dating games #1:

First Date

MELODY CARLSON

Revell

a division of Baker Publishing Group
Grand Rapids, Michigan

Published by Revell
a division of Baker Publishing Group
P.O. Box 6287, Grand Rapids, MI 49516-6287
www.revellbooks.com

Printed in the United States of America

Library of Congress Cataloging-in-Publication Data is on file at the Library of Congress, Washington, DC.

ISBN 978-0-8007-2131-2

This is a work of fiction. Names, characters, incidents, and dialogues are products of the author's imagination and are not to be construed as real. Any resemblance to actual events or persons, living or dead, is entirely coincidental.

Scripture used in this book, whether quoted or paraphrased by the characters, is taken from The Holy Bible, English Standard Version® (ESV®), copyright © 2001 by Crossway, a publishing ministry of Good News Publishers. Used by permission. All rights reserved. ESV Text Edition: 2007

13 14 15 16 17 18 19   7 6 5 4 3 2 1

Two weeks into her junior year and Devon Fremont felt dangerously bored. Okay, *bored* (or the *b*-word, as her mom would say) was an understatement—Devon felt like she was sleepwalking. Anyway, she reminded herself as she strolled through the well-maintained Northwood Academy courtyard, she was still the "new girl" on campus. That alone should make life interesting. Acclimating to a new high school, new friends, new classes, pretty much new everything . . . this was not the formula for boredom. And yet Devon felt something was missing. She decided it was high time to stir things up.

"This school is too freaking quiet," Devon complained to Emma Parks as they met at their usual pre-lunch spot beneath the massive oak tree in the courtyard. Devon glanced over to where several girls were clustered on a nearby bench. Looking about in a listless sort of way, they seemed bored too. A couple guys were strolling straight toward them, but based on their blank expressions, either the girls were invisible or these guys were from another planet. Or zombies.

"Seriously, what is up with this place?" Devon asked Emma.

"Huh?" Emma's pale blue eyes squinted in the autumn sunlight. "What do you mean?" Emma had been Devon's best friend for ages and was one of the main reasons Devon had transferred to Northwood this year. Well, to be more accurate, it was because of Emma *and* Devon's mom. After her divorce became final last spring, Mom had become unexplainably paranoid that her only child was going to get into serious trouble before graduating high school. For that reason she'd insisted it was time for Devon to exit the public school system and come here.

"What are you yammering about now?" Emma asked as they walked toward the cafeteria together.

"I just want to know why everyone at Northwood is so totally subdued," Devon said. "This place feels more like a morgue than a high school."

"That's ridiculous," Emma said defensively. "Just because Northwood's not as chaotic and crazy as BHS doesn't mean it's a morgue."

"Like you can even remember what Brewster was like," Devon challenged. "You were there for about two weeks before your mom yanked you out. And that was like three years ago."

"Well, two weeks was more than enough. The place was a zoo."

"Yeah, and zoos are fun." Devon hadn't even told Emma about some of the crazy events she'd been part of back at BHS.

Emma pushed open the door. "If it's any comfort, I do remember being upset when I first came here too. But really, it didn't take long before I got it. This is a great school, Devon. Just give it a chance."

"I suppose it's great if you don't mind being in an old folks' home. Maybe we should all be wearing our Depends."

Emma let out a groan as she rolled her eyes. *"Puh-leeze."*

As they walked through the cafeteria, Devon glanced around the partially filled tables and chairs. This space was only slightly more active than the courtyard, although that may have been because people were occupied with eating. "Seriously, Em, it's like everyone here is in a stupor . . . or a coma . . . or maybe they've been sneaking into their moms' Xanax."

Emma flopped her purse on their usual table. "Very funny." She shook her head dismally.

"What's very funny?" Cassidy asked as Devon hung her bag on the back of a vacant chair. Emma and her friends claimed this table for lunch every day. And while Devon was grateful to be included in their little clique, she wished these girls were a bit more adventuresome.

"Devon's just making fun of our school again," Emma explained with an irritated edge to her voice. "She thinks we're all on sedatives."

"Huh?" Abby looked up from her phone. "You're calling us addicts now?"

"No," Devon clarified. "It's just that this place is so quiet. I mean, compared to my old school."

Cassidy gave Devon a dismal look. "You still claim you'd rather go to school with a bunch of gangsters than get a good education here at Northwood? Seriously?"

Devon was still getting used to these girls, but she had the least tolerance for Miss Goody-Two-Shoes, aka Cassidy Banks. She was pretty sure the feelings were mutual too. Originally Devon assumed this personality conflict was because Cassidy and Emma had been such good friends last year, before Devon showed up and took over. It was natural for Cassidy to resent Devon. But didn't she realize that Devon and Emma had been best friends since forever?

Devon eyed Cassidy. "Is there some reason we can't get a good education and have a good time too? Or is that too much to ask of this preppy school?"

Cassidy shrugged in her superior way. "Well, I guess high school is what you make of it. Maybe you haven't tried hard enough."

As Devon followed Emma over to the food court, she thought about Cassidy's answer. It sounded like an invitation for Devon to stir something up. Maybe she would. As she filled her soda cup with ice, Devon noticed Harris Martin just a few feet away. This tall, sandy-haired dude had caught her eye on her first day here. He reminded her of Matthew McConaughey. Right now he was reaching for a cheeseburger and saying something under his breath to his buddy Isaac. They both laughed at whatever witty thing Harris had murmured, and, completely oblivious to Devon's blatant interest in them, the guys continued on toward the cashier without even a sideways glance. What was up with them?

Devon had been trying to get Harris's attention for more than a week now. So far, she'd only managed to catch a semi-interested glance that she'd hoped had been cast in her direction but might've just as easily been aimed at something else. She wasn't used to being ignored like this. She caught her image in the mirrored wall behind the salad bar. Maybe she'd missed something this morning. But her long, thick hair seemed to be in place—some people called her a redhead, but she preferred to say auburn. Her shirt seemed to show off the curves that nature had endowed her with. Even her lip gloss looked fresh.

In the last year, Devon hadn't had any problem catching a guy's eye when she wanted—sometimes even when she didn't. She'd even had some guys following her around at her previous school. Sure, they weren't the guys she was hoping for, but she'd enjoyed stringing them along. However, she had saved her best flirty moves and smiles for the guys who mattered. Unfortunately, her efforts appeared to be lost on Harris. Was it just him? Or was she losing her appeal altogether?

By the time she and Emma rejoined their friends, Devon was actually starting to question herself. What if she really had lost something? Or perhaps she just wasn't the kind of girl that interested guys at Northwood. She bit her lip as she set her tray down. Maybe she wasn't as hot as she'd imagined.

"What's wrong with you now?" Cassidy demanded of Devon.

"Huh?" Devon sat down.

"You look really perplexed," Abby said.

"What—were they out of chili fries or something?" Cassidy teased.

The girls laughed like this was humorous.

"I *am* perplexed," Devon admitted in a grumpy tone. "I mean, what does it take to get a guy's attention around here? What's up with these Northwood boys anyway? Don't they like girls?"

Her friends laughed harder, and now several slams and

insults were tossed Devon's way. That's what you get for being honest.

"Maybe you're just not their type," Bryn Jacobs teased. Of course, this was easy for Bryn to say. With her gorgeous mane of naturally blonde hair and those big blue eyes, she was always turning heads. However, as far as Devon knew, Bryn had never had a regular boyfriend either. She didn't even seem to date. Really, what was up with that?

"I'm serious," Devon told Bryn. "I'm not used to being ignored like this. Are these guys broken or blind or what?"

"Get over yourself," Cassidy said impatiently. "Just because our Northwood guys don't act like those hormone-driven Brewster boys doesn't mean there's something wrong with them. It just means they have better manners."

"But it's a Friday," Devon pointed out, "with a whole weekend ahead of us. Shouldn't these guys be thinking about something besides school and sports? What about dating? Don't they even *like* girls? It's as if someone has medicated them so that they can't even see us girls."

Bryn giggled. "Trust me. They can see us."

"I'm not so sure." Devon shook her head. "Something is fishy. Seventeen- and eighteen-year-old guys who aren't into girls? There is something seriously wrong with that. It's not normal."

As Devon dug into her salad, the table grew quiet, and she couldn't tell if the girls were thinking about what she'd just said or simply concentrating on their lunches and cell phones. Maybe no one cared.

"I'll tell you what's going on," Emma said quietly.

"Going on with what?" Cassidy asked.

"With the guys in this school." Emma glanced around as if to be sure no one was around to eavesdrop.

Devon frowned doubtfully at her shy friend. "Are you saying you know why these guys are so uninterested in girls?" How could Emma possibly get this? Her experience with boys was so minimal it was laughable. However, Devon knew better than to tease her best friend.

"I'll tell you guys what I think is going on," Emma continued in a hushed tone. "But only if you promise not to repeat it."

Now she had the attention of all the girls. They'd stopped eating and were leaning toward Emma with interest, giving their word that they wouldn't tell, but now Emma looked uncertain.

"Come on," Devon pressed. "Spill the beans. What's up with these guys? Inquiring minds want to know."

"Well, I should probably keep my mouth shut . . . but I remember something Edward said a couple years ago—about this speech the guys are given at the start of the school year. Only the junior and senior guys get to hear it."

"Huh?" Bryn frowned. "Who's Edward?"

"Emma's older brother," Devon explained quickly. Why didn't Bryn know this? "What kind of speech, Em?"

"Well, I obviously didn't *hear* the speech, but I did overhear Edward and his buddy talking about it. It seems that Mr. Worthington always gives the older guys this little talk. It's a Northwood tradition."

"What kind of talk?" Bryn demanded.

"From what I can tell it has to do with respecting girls. Worthington talks to them about dating and that kind of stuff. I think he challenges the guys to accept a code of honor. I'm not sure, but I do remember that Edward took it pretty seriously in his senior year. He even chose *not* to date at all . . . well, at least for a while anyway."

"Good for him," Cassidy said. "Dating is like asking for trouble."

"Hey, I remember your brother dated Shandra Tompkins before he graduated," Abby pointed out. "What was up with that?"

"That's true," Emma admitted. "But that was after he'd gone for most of the school year without a single date. I'm just about positive it was because of that little talk."

"Maybe Worthington's talk is kind of like the guys' version of the purity pledge," Cassidy said with enthusiasm. "You know, like the one we took at church back in middle school. Remember?"

"You took a purity pledge?" Devon asked Cassidy.

Cassidy looked uneasy. "Didn't you?"

Devon frowned. "No . . ."

"Never mind." Cassidy shrugged as she reached for her water bottle.

"Anyway," Emma jumped back in. "That might explain why the guys are acting kinda chilly toward you . . . and the other girls."

Devon watched Emma push a strand of drab, dishwater blonde hair out of her eyes. If Devon had her way, she would've given her best friend a makeover by now. However, Emma had already declined the offer—several times. Still, it wasn't easy having a ho-hum looking best friend, and it certainly didn't help the less than warm dating atmosphere here at Northwood. Especially if what Emma was describing was true. A code of honor? How boring was that?

"Well, at least we know what's going on now," Bryn said in a dismal tone. "Why we're being ignored like this. The guys are just trying to be honorable."

"That's nice," Cassidy said. "I like it."

"It makes sense," Abby conceded. "Especially since everyone respects Mr. Worthington. I can understand how a speech from him might make guys think twice about dating."

"It does take the pressure off," Bryn said. "If no one's dating, it's no big deal, right?"

"Maybe it's no big deal right now." The wheels in Devon's head were turning. "But what if things start to change?"

"What's going to change?" Abby asked.

"The girls." Devon gave her friends a sly smile.

"How so?" Bryn asked.

"The girls didn't hear old Worthington's speech, did they?" Devon was putting together a plan as she spoke.

"Well, no, but—"

"That means we girls don't have to accept whatever it is that Worthington told them. Do we?"

"Of course we have to accept it," Cassidy challenged. "Why wouldn't we accept it?"

"Because it's no fun." Devon eyed the girls, wondering how game they'd be. "It's just plain boring. And I, for one, refuse to go along with it. I want to have some fun this year."

Abby's dark eyes flickered with interest. "So what are you going to do about it?"

"I have a plan."

"Let's hear it," Bryn urged.

Devon slowly looked around the table, studying this diverse mix of five girls. Being new to the group, she wasn't sure what the common denominator was that connected them as friends, or even how long they'd been friends. At first she'd assumed it was church they had in common, but now she knew that wasn't exactly right because not everyone in this group attended church. Still, they seemed to be a solid clique, and for now, thanks to Emma, she was part of it—and grateful for it. Even so, she knew they could be having more fun, if only someone would lead the way. That was where she came in.

"Come on," Abby begged her. "Out with it. Let's hear your plan."

"Well, I'm not even sure if it would interest *all* of you . . ." Devon purposely kept her voice quiet and somewhat mysterious. "But I was imagining a plan . . . or maybe it's more like a game. Or a game plan." She laughed.

"What is it?" Bryn asked curiously.

"It's something that could be pretty cool, and something we could do together." She was about to add that it would bring real excitement to their blasé little lives, but she knew that would sound too demeaning, and she didn't want to alienate any of them—particularly Cassidy, who would probably turn out to be a big wet blanket.

"What are you talking about?" Cassidy's brow was already creased with suspicion. "What kind of game plan?"

Devon made what she hoped was an enticing smile. "First, let me ask all of you something."

"Ask away," Bryn said.

"It's about guys," Devon told her. "Before I tell you my game plan, I have a question for everyone—about dating."

"What?" Abby's eyes glimmered with interest.

"When was the last time you were on a date?" Devon scanned the girls. "I mean a *real* date." She pointed at Emma. "You don't even need to answer because I know you've never been on a date before." The table got very quiet, and Devon could tell she'd made the others uncomfortable. But she didn't care. At least she was stirring things up.

Devon felt slightly guilty about her question when she noticed that Emma's fair cheeks had turned pink with embarrassment. Of course, Devon knew that Emma had never dated. Everyone knew that. Poor Emma had never even had a boy look twice at her. She just looked down at her tray and said nothing.

"Hey, it's okay." Devon patted Emma's shoulder. "I'm sure you're not alone. Especially in this school. So, anyway, how about the rest of you? Who here has dated much? Or has ever dated at all?"

"I *don't* date," Cassidy proclaimed with what sounded like pride. "By choice."

"Really?" Devon pressed her lips together and slowly shook her head. She wanted to challenge this by asking whose choice it was—Cassidy's, or the guys who were uninterested in going out with such a boring-looking girl. Oh, Cass was okay looking with her long, dark hair, but she did absolutely nothing to enhance her appearance. Naturally, Devon kept her mouth shut and her thoughts to herself. She needed Cassidy's approval in order to make her game plan work. Whether it was said or not, Cassidy played a strong role as a leader in this group of girls. Perhaps that was just one more reason Cassidy resented Devon.

"The truth is, my parents wouldn't let me date," Bryn admitted. "Not until I turned sixteen, that is."

"But you turned sixteen last summer," Abby reminded her.

"Yeah." Bryn narrowed her eyes. "And your point is?"

"Well . . . you haven't gone out since your birthday and—"

"You've never had a real date either," Bryn said hotly.

"At least I had a boyfriend and I—"

"If you call holding hands with Lewis Snipes 'having a boyfriend,' then—"

"Hey—hey!" Devon held up her hands. "It's not like I'm trying to start a war here. I was just curious. Anyway, your answers have me convinced I was right."

"Right about what?" Cassidy demanded.

"That some of you might want to play this game with me." Devon waited.

"Huh?" Emma looked confused.

"What game?" Abby asked.

"Come on," Bryn urged. "Enough of the mystique, Devon. Stop talking in circles and just tell us about your game or your plan or whatever it is."

Devon took in a slow breath. It was actually something that had occurred to her in a split-second flash—and she wasn't even sure she'd fully wrapped her head around it yet. But wasn't brilliance like that sometimes? Straight out of the blue? "Okay, this is the deal. I want to create a secret club," she declared, "for girls like us."

"What do you mean, *girls like us*?" Cassidy asked.

"Girls who haven't dated," Devon clarified.

"A secret club?" Emma looked bewildered but interested.

"I'm calling it the Dating Games club," Devon said quickly. She was making this up as she went along, but it seemed to make sense. Besides, this was the most fun she'd had since starting school here. And really, what harm could it do?

"Dating Games?" Abby tilted her head to one side. "How does it work?"

"For starters, we all have to agree to join the club and that we'll keep it a secret. Because if the word got out, it would spoil everything."

"What exactly does this 'secret' dating club do?" Cassidy demanded. "If you ask me, it sounds skanky. And I refuse to join a club that's going to—"

"It will not be skanky," Devon assured her. "It'll be a way for us to ease ourselves into the dating game. To start with, we'll help each other to better ourselves." She glanced nervously at Emma. "Then we'll help each other to get to know some guys. Don't worry, I mean *nice* guys. The goal will be to help each other to get into the dating game too. We'll do it as a group. But we must keep the club under wraps. And as members of this club, we must take care of each other—you know, watch each other's backs." She smiled in satisfaction. This was actually sounding pretty good. "Because you know what they say," she said as if concluding a speech. "There's safety in numbers."

"I sort of get that." Bryn nodded eagerly. "Cool idea, Devon."

"I like that we help each other." Abby held up her water bottle with enthusiasm. "Here's to sisterhood and to dating. When do we start?"

"Hold on there." Cassidy still looked doubtful.

Ignoring her, Emma started to ask questions. "But we'll *all* date, right? And we'll only date nice guys—is that what you're saying, Devon?" She looked hopeful and slightly eager.

"Absolutely," Devon assured her.

"But how can you promise—"

"We'll make some rules." Devon cut Cassidy off. "To make sure we do this in the best possible way. And I already know what the first rule will be. 'No girl left behind.'"

"What's that supposed to mean?" Cassidy demanded.

"No one goes out with a guy until all the girls in the club have a date lined up. It's a group deal. We're in this together." Devon let out a satisfied sigh. This was even better than she'd initially imagined. She felt like a dating genius. Maybe she'd patent this thing or start a reality show.

"All right." Bryn gave her a solid thumbs-up. "Count me in."

"Me too." Abby grinned.

"Okay . . ." Emma made a nervous smile. "Then I'm in too."

"Just like that?" Cassidy frowned at them like they'd lost their senses. "You cannot possibly be serious."

"You don't want to join the club?" Devon feigned disappointment, but the truth was, she didn't care whether Cassidy joined or not. If there was one girl who needed to be left behind, it had to be Miss Goody-Two-Shoes. She could be such a buzzkill.

"I don't think so." Cassidy looked perplexed.

Instead of cheering, Devon sadly shook her head. "Well, five girls seemed like a good number for the DG. But maybe four is better—"

"Hey, I'll bet Felicia will want to join." Bryn reached for

her phone. "She's at the orthodontist right now, but I can send her a text and—"

"Wait." Emma pointed back at Cassidy. "Are you absolutely positive you don't want in, Cass? Because I think we could use someone sensible like you in this club."

"I don't know . . ." Cassidy looked slightly torn now.

"It'll be fun," Bryn said. "And Devon's right. We do need to do something to liven things up around here. Besides, homecoming isn't far off. What about the dance? Wouldn't it be fun to go with a real date?"

The other girls began talking enthusiastically, encouraging Cassidy to give this club a try. Devon tried to appear supportive too, but the truth was, this whole thing would probably go much more smoothly without Cassidy's constant whining and complaining.

"Seriously, Cass, do you plan to sit home by yourself while the rest of us are at the homecoming dance with our dates?" Bryn demanded.

Cassidy rolled her eyes with skepticism. "Like you will all have dates by then."

"What if we do have dates?" Emma said quietly.

"Maybe I should just call Felicia?" Bryn held up her phone as if to threaten Cassidy.

"Come on, Cassidy," Emma said. "If I'm willing to try this, you should be too."

"It's complicated." Cassidy bit her lip. "I mean, like I already told you guys, I kind of decided not to date. I made a commitment last spring."

"To who?" Bryn asked.

"To myself."

"Well, undo the commitment," Abby urged. "Live a little."

"When you made this commitment"—Devon frowned—"I mean, *not* to date . . . who was asking you out? Was there a line of guys at your door or something?"

The others laughed, but Cassidy glared at Devon. "There were some possibilities."

Devon forced a smile. "Yeah, of course. But what made you decide you didn't want to date? I'm just curious."

"I'd read something about it." Cassidy pushed a long strand of dark brown hair over her shoulder. She wasn't the prettiest girl of the bunch, but some guys might find her attractive in that wholesome girl-next-door sort of way. "Anyway, it seemed like a sensible idea."

"So you'll never date? Not ever?" Bryn looked disappointed.

"I told my dad that I wasn't going to start dating until I turned eighteen," Cassidy confided. "He was really happy about it."

"Of course he was happy." Devon shook her head. "He's your father. What did you expect? Most dads would like their daughters to put off dating until they're thirty."

"But how realistic is that?" Bryn challenged.

"Besides, like Devon said, a club will be a *safe* way for us to date," Abby said encouragingly to Cassidy. "Your dad might even approve."

"I've heard stories about overprotected girls who don't date in high school and then go off to college and fall apart completely," Abby pointed out. "Some of them get pregnant or worse—"

"What's worse than getting pregnant?" Emma asked.

"Being slipped ecstasy, or date rape, or—"

"Okay, we're getting sidetracked," Bryn interjected.

"Not really," Abby protested. "When girls are totally clueless when it comes to guys, they probably set themselves up for trouble."

"Which is precisely why I don't date," Cassidy said victoriously.

"Yes, but wouldn't it be better to learn about guys *now*?" Devon asked her. "Right here in the safety of a friendly club and a Christian high school?"

"Yeah," Emma said with more confidence. "I think so too. It makes perfect sense to me."

"I agree," Bryn said. "Count me in."

"Me too," Abby chimed in.

"Great." Devon smiled triumphantly. "That makes four of us. That should be enough."

"Unless we invite Felicia," Bryn reminded her.

"You're really not joining?" Emma looked at Cassidy with concerned eyes. "You won't even try?"

Cassidy looked around the table with uncertainty. "You said there'd be rules," she said cautiously to Devon. "What exactly *are* the rules?"

"We'll have to make them," Devon explained. "Together. After all, it's a club. All the members would have to agree on the rules."

"So I'd have a say in making the rules?" Cassidy looked slightly hopeful.

"Sure." Devon made an uneasy smile. She couldn't act like she didn't want Cassidy to join, but she'd been relieved to think Cassidy was bowing out. "We'll have to sit down and make the rules together."

"But not right now." Abby pointed to the oversized watch on her slender, cocoa brown wrist. "It's almost time for class."

As if to confirm this, the bell rang.

"How about if we meet again after school," Cassidy suggested. "I have jazz choir until five, but we can meet at—"

Devon interrupted, saying she'd text the others with the location and coordinate the time. No way was she going to let Cassidy take the lead in this. After all, it was her idea. Cassidy hadn't even been interested. Devon was not going to let that bossy girl get the upper hand. Fortunately, no one seemed to question her.

Devon felt triumphant as she walked to her next class—at least until she spotted Harris and Isaac standing by the trophy case outside of the administration center. As usual, the boys continued to act like she didn't exist. Instead of looking her way, the two of them were joking around with some of their guy friends. However, as she got closer, she thought she observed a couple of quick glances tossed in her direction. It might have been her hopeful imagination, but just in case, she flipped her hair over her shoulder like an auburn flag, held her chin high, and strutted along with a flirty little bounce in her step. Might as well remind them of what they were missing out on.

As she whooshed past the group of boys, she had to suppress the urge to giggle at their naïve oblivion. Because, if she had her way, it wouldn't be long until those very guys would be wondering what hit them. Let the Dating Games begin.

C assidy still felt torn. On one hand, she was curious about Devon's new idea, and although she didn't want to admit it, especially not to Devon, it sounded kind of fun. On the other hand, a dating club could turn into a real train wreck. As she waited for the final bell to ring, having finished this week's civics test with ample time to spare, she pondered all that had been said at lunch. The more she thought about it, the more she knew it made absolutely no sense to participate in Devon's stupid scheme.

Really, what would her parents think if she suddenly announced that she wanted to date guys? Dad had been so proud of her for being "such a sensible girl." And the *sensible* thing would be to simply nip this nonsense in the bud. She would tell her friends in no uncertain terms that the Dating Games club was a bad idea, that she had no intention of being involved, and that if they were smart, they wouldn't either. The end.

Cassidy had been nurturing doubts about Devon Fremont

from the get-go. She'd only met Devon once before the school year—through Emma—but based on some of the stories Emma had shared, Devon was trouble. When Cassidy learned that Devon was transferring to Northwood, she'd felt her guard going up. She hadn't wanted to step away from her friendship with Emma, but it seemed clear that Devon had already staked her claim there. At the time Cassidy simply told herself that she didn't need a best friend. She was used to being something of a loner. She called it independence. Plus she had God. If Devon needed Emma by her side, why should Cassidy try to stop her?

Yet she was unsure. Perhaps she was being disloyal to Emma, but something about Devon definitely bugged Cassidy. It wasn't that she was jealous either. Something about the fast-talking, fun-seeking, showy redhead had roused her suspicions right from the start. If Devon hadn't been such good friends with Emma, Cassidy never would've befriended her at all. Not that they were exactly friends, but she'd tried to be civil to Devon. It was the Christian thing to do.

But then Devon tossed out this stupid Dating Games idea. *Seriously?* No, Cassidy's mind was made up—she was definitely out. The sooner she told her friends, the better. She let out a sigh of relief and looked at the clock—and that was when she noticed Lane Granger sitting two seats ahead of her. Lane was jiggling his number 2 pencil between his fingers and watching the clock too. Like her, he'd finished the test early. But then she always knew he was smart.

Cassidy stared at the back of Lane's blue plaid shirt, admiring how perfectly it fit over his broad squared shoulders. She also liked the way his dark brown hair waved so attractively around his perfectly shaped ears. She sighed inwardly. She'd been secretly crushing on this guy since the beginning of her sophomore year. Unfortunately, Lane didn't even know she existed. Okay, that was an overstatement. They'd been on various committees together last year. They'd even had some brief conversations. Still, it was like they lived on different planets.

And yet . . . maybe not. After all, they did share some commonalities. Like her, Lane was comfortable in taking on roles that involved leadership. The interesting thing was that when Lane was in charge of a committee, Cassidy was suddenly able to follow. With Lane at the helm, she was content to take a backseat. Even if she wound up flipping pancakes or filling balloons with helium, if Lane was giving the orders, she would gladly take them. The problem was, once the project ended, she never got more than a polite nod or a friendly "hey" from the attractive senior.

Cassidy pressed her lips together, thinking carefully now. Had she missed something? What if Devon's weird Dating Games club could somehow secure Cassidy a date with Lane Granger? Wouldn't that be enough to change her opinion on dating . . . and Devon? Cassidy knew that Lane attended a church. Not hers, unfortunately. But she'd been watching him long enough and closely enough to know that he was one of the good guys. And as far as she could tell, and to her huge relief, he wasn't dating anyone in particular. Maybe she'd made up her mind about Devon too quickly. She knew she had a tendency to be overly judgmental. What if the DG club could actually work?

Cassidy watched as Lane leaned over to reach for his backpack, and as he turned in his seat, their eyes met and a warm rush ran through her. Instead of looking away, like Cassidy was tempted to do, Lane kept his eyes steadily on her—almost as if he was actually seeing her! Was it really possible? When he finally turned away, she could feel her face flushing and a strange fluttery feeling inside of her chest. She took a deep breath to steady herself. Wow!

Okay, maybe she needed to rethink her ideas about dating. She wondered how long Lane's single status would last. Especially since he was often surrounded by girls. Plus, as a senior, he probably could have his pick of the girls in the school. She'd always assumed his female buddies were from his church because they all seemed like solid friends who had known each other for years. But it seemed likely that some of those girls, just like Cassidy, were hoping to be more than just friends.

At times she'd imagined ways she could break into Lane's social circle. She'd even considered visiting his church, but that felt a little like stalking, so she had simply admired him from afar. Really, it seemed that Lane Granger was meant to be only a pleasant fantasy for her. That is . . . unless . . . maybe this was the year that would change. Maybe she and Lane could finally—

Her daydream was smacked back to reality by the ringing of the release bell. As she scrambled to grab her test paper and gather her stuff, she made up her mind. Just like that, she knew she was in. As she followed Lane to the front of the room and dropped her test right on top of his, she couldn't wait to go to Devon's meeting today. If Devon could convince her (starting with a reasonable set of rules) that the Dating Games club was not going to be skanky or stupid or sleazy, Cassidy would join. Besides, she assured herself as she walked toward her locker, she could always drop out if she didn't like how it was headed. In the meantime, she could watch out for Emma and her other friends. Really, part of her reasoning was selfless and altruistic.

After she exchanged some books at her locker, she checked her phone and saw that Devon had already texted her. The plan was for everyone to meet at Costello's Coffee at 5:00. As she walked toward the music department, she texted a confirmation back to Devon. Feeling like she was about to embark on an exciting adventure, she went into the choir room where the jazz choir was already gathered. They were expected to rehearse after school every day until the jazz concert in three weeks. Mr. Spencer was already at the piano, and Cassidy quickly found her place with the other sopranos. Singing in choir was the only nonacademic activity she truly excelled in. Being picked for jazz choir on the second day of school had been the highlight of her year so far. As a result, she always gave these practices 100 percent—and more, if that was possible.

However, she realized as they were wrapping up, she'd only given the music 90 percent of her energy today. The missing 10 percent was due to the distracting thoughts of Lane Granger that were still dancing through her head. That, combined with the hopes that this Dating Games club was going to change her life, had caused her to give less than her best effort in jazz choir. As she walked to her car, she felt sincerely embarrassed. Why was she turning into such a little fool? Wouldn't she be totally humiliated if anyone knew what she'd been thinking about these last couple of hours? What had happened to the usual sensible Cassidy Banks? Maybe that was what boys did to a girl.

And yet . . . maybe it was because she was usually such a

practical, down-to-earth, and sensible girl, but it was surprisingly fun to entertain these unexpected ponderings about a boy. Even if this was just a brief interlude, it was still amusing. She reassured herself that she could still pull the plug on this Dating Games club—possibly for everyone's sake. Perhaps that was the only reason she was going to meet them at Costello's. At least that was what she told herself.

She unlocked her car, a white Toyota with nearly 150,000 miles on it. It was nearly as old as she was but as dependable as her father. Dad had surprised her with this car last spring, not long after she'd secured her driver's license and not long after she'd told Dad about her plans to postpone dating and romance until she finished high school. Whether it was getting her license or her consistent good grades or that particular announcement that had landed her a car, she could never be sure. But she felt reasonably certain that Dad wouldn't take the car away from her if she went on a date. That wasn't his style.

Although her parents encouraged her to honor God with how she lived her life, they also allowed her to make her own decisions. Well, about most things. Sometimes they intervened, but they didn't usually need to because Cassidy was normally as levelheaded as (sometimes even more than) most adults. That was exactly why, before she started her car, she called her mom and left a message that she would be home a little bit later because she was meeting friends for coffee at Costello's. Naturally she didn't go into the details of this coffee date. Perhaps she would tell Mom later, after she decided it was not a good idea, and they would laugh about it together.

Cassidy fastened her seat belt, checked her mirrors, and

carefully backed up. Dad had warned her more than once that it was the overconfident drivers who caused the most wrecks. "Pride comes before the crash," he would jokingly tell her. She'd also signed a pact never to text while driving—and she took it as seriously as she took her pledge not to have sex until marriage. While a pledge like that might've been an oddity in schools like Brewster High, where Devon used to go, Cassidy believed it was probably the norm at Northwood Academy. It comforted her to know this. Their high school was like a safe zone, a haven in a wild and crazy world.

As expected, Cassidy was the last one to arrive at Costello's. "Did I miss anything?" she asked as she joined them with her mocha in hand.

"Nothing much," Emma said quickly.

"Ha!" Bryn elbowed Emma. "Only that our little Emma has been crushing on a particular guy."

"Really?" Cassidy found this hard to believe. Shy, quiet Emma had actually admitted to something like this? She sat down. "Who?"

"No one," Emma snapped. "They're delusional."

"So if Isaac McKinley asked you to homecoming, you'd tell him to go take a hike?" Devon said in a teasing tone.

Emma rolled her eyes, but Cassidy could tell by her flushed cheeks that she was actually embarrassed. "Really?" Cassidy pressed. "You like Isaac?"

Emma just shrugged, then looked down at her drink.

"See," Devon proclaimed. "This is exactly why we need the DG. Emma needs our help." She patted Emma's back. "That's what friends are for."

Emma gave her a meek smile. "Just don't make fun of me, okay?"

"Okay." Devon nodded. "In fact, we should probably have that in our rules. No making fun of each other when it comes to dating or anyone's taste in guys."

Everyone seemed to agree with Devon. In fact, the rest of them seemed surprisingly agreeable—and it was clear that Devon had taken the lead.

"So you started making rules without me?" Cassidy was trying not to feel too left out, but it wasn't easy. She looked around the table, wondering how she really fit in with this mix of girls. First there was the gorgeous blonde Bryn, a way too fashion-driven but relatively nice girl who could sometimes act like an airhead. Then there was Abby with her flawless dark skin, sleek black hair, fabulous smile—smart and fun and witty. And even though the flashy Devon with her red hair and exuberant ways got to Cass, she knew that Devon was out of her league when it came to attracting boys. Really, Emma was the only one Cassidy felt truly comfortable with. She was fairly ordinary looking with her dishwater blonde hair and a plain gray hoodie. Until Devon came along, Cassidy and Emma had been best friends. "I thought we were all in this together," Cassidy said quietly. Maybe they'd rather she hadn't come.

"Don't worry, we were waiting for you," Bryn assured her.

"Did you bring your iPad?" Abby asked. "We voted unanimously for you to be our secretary."

"Really?" Cassidy blinked as she reached for her bag.

"Do you mind?" Devon asked in a surprisingly polite way.

"No, that's okay." Caught off guard by their warmth, Cassidy pulled out her iPad. "So is that a real rule?" she asked. "No making fun of each other?" She started to type it out.

"Maybe we could say it in a more positive way," Abby suggested. "In speech class, we've been focusing on rephrasing ourselves to sound positive."

"How would you say it?" Cassidy paused, ready to hit Delete.

Bryn got a thoughtful look. "How about we say something about loyalty instead?"

"How do we want to word this?" Cassidy asked. "I mean, you probably don't want to say it like the Ten Commandments. 'Thou shalt be loyal to thy friends'?"

They laughed.

"No, that's a little stiff," Abby told her.

"How about the Girl Scout Law," Cassidy said. "I will do my best to be loyal to my—"

"No, no, no," Bryn insisted. "I have bad memories of Girl Scouts."

Cassidy wanted to argue this point but realized it wouldn't get their rules written. Instead she focused on the keyboard, typing out a short simple sentence. "How about this? 'We will be loyal to each other.'"

A few more suggestions and tweaks were made and finally, Cassidy read the first rule. "We will be loyal to our friends in the DG." She looked at them. "Does that sound all right?"

They all agreed, and now Devon suggested the next rule. "We will help our friends in the DG to find dates."

"Dates with good guys," Emma added.

Cassidy typed this in. "We will help our friends in the DG to find dates with good guys," she told them.

"How do we define *good*?" Abby asked. "Good looking? Good at sports? Good in—"

"Not that kind of good," Emma said. "Good in character. We don't want anyone in the DG to date a jerk. Right?"

"Right," Bryn echoed.

"Absolutely," Devon said.

They continued suggesting rules, going over them, agreeing on some, and dumping others. Eventually they had a set of ten rules. They weren't exactly the Ten Commandments, but there were some similarities. Although she didn't point this out. She didn't want them to laugh at her again.

"Go ahead and read the rules," Devon told Cassidy.

Cassidy read:

Dating Games Club Rules

1. We will honor the secret membership of the DG.
2. We will be loyal to our fellow DG members.
3. We will help fellow DG members to find dates with good guys.
4. We will report back to the DG regarding our dates.
5. We will not be jealous over a fellow DG member's boyfriend.
6. We will never steal a fellow DG member's boyfriend.
7. We will abstain from sex on our DG dates.
8. We will not lie to the DG about what happens on our dates.
9. We will never let a boyfriend come between fellow DG members.
10. We will admit new DG members only by unanimous vote.

"That sounds perfect," Devon told Cassidy. "You make a really good secretary!"

Cassidy thanked her, wondering if she'd judged Devon too harshly. Really, she was pretty nice. And the DG rules sounded fair and smart. Nothing to suggest this might turn sleazy or skanky. All very reassuring.

"If Cassidy's secretary, who's president?" Bryn asked.

"Devon, of course," Abby told her. "It was her idea."

"But shouldn't we vote?"

They voted, and since there was no opposition, Devon was unanimously elected president of the DG. However, although Cassidy had voted for Devon and started seeing her in a better light, she still wasn't completely convinced. If she hadn't already been appointed secretary, she might've made a run for this office herself, which made her wonder if Devon hadn't set it up like that on purpose. Although it was possible that Cassidy was just being suspicious. Why not hope for the best and just see how it went?

"Do you want me to make an acceptance speech?" Devon teased.

"Sure," Bryn told her.

"I was just kidding."

"I want to hear a speech," Cassidy insisted.

"Yeah, go for it," Abby urged.

"Okay." Devon's brow creased as if she was thinking. "As your new president of the newly formed DG, I promise to devote myself to seriously improving your love life—I mean your *dating* life." She giggled. "As your president, I promise that by the homecoming dance, we will all have dates. Or else I'll resign as your leader."

"That's a big promise," Cassidy told her. "I mean, it's only about three weeks until homecoming."

"Yeah," Emma agreed. "Maybe we should give this a little more time."

"I didn't promise we'd all have a perfect date," Devon said with a mischievous grin. "We might have to do a little settling while we're getting the kinks worked out of the club. But we'll just consider it good practice, right?"

Cassidy wasn't so sure. "Are you saying I'll have to go out with a guy I don't really like?"

Devon shrugged. "I'm saying we should be open to the possibilities. After all, it's called the Dating *Games*. Doesn't that suggest that we should be open to playing with it a little?"

"But no jerks," Emma reminded her.

"Yeah, yeah." Devon waved a hand. "No jerks."

Cassidy was still concerned. "But what if I don't like the guy you find for me to go—"

"Come on, Cass," Devon said casually. "So what if your first date *isn't* your dream guy? It's not the end of the world, is it? I mean, it's not like you're going to marry him and have his babies—are you?"

The others laughed and Cassidy tried to act like it was humorous, but at the same time she resented Devon making fun of her.

"Anyway, I think we made real progress. Now I think we should promise to uphold these rules." Devon held up her hand as if to make a pledge. "You guys in?"

Cassidy glanced around the coffeehouse to see if anyone was watching them, but other than the barista and an elderly couple in the far corner, the place was pretty much empty. She wasn't even sure why she cared.

"I know it's kind of silly," Devon admitted, "but if we're going to take the DG seriously, I think we should all make the same pledge."

So right there, at a back table in Costello's Coffee, they all pledged to uphold the Dating Games rules.

"Let the games begin." Devon held up her coffee cup like

she was giving a toast. The others did the same, clicking their cups together. "Now we need to make it clear which guys we're setting our sights on. Like I said, let's not go to pieces if we don't score a first date with our Mr. Right just yet. But at least we'll all know who we're aiming at. That way we can work together." She pointed to herself. "I'll begin. I've got my eye on Harris Martin."

Bryn's big blue eyes widened in surprise, and although she didn't mention it, Cassidy wondered if Bryn might've had her eye on the same guy. Harris Martin was considered one of the hottest guys in school.

"We know that Emma is interested in Isaac." Devon grinned at Emma. "Which is pretty convenient."

"I kind of like Kent Renner," Abby told them.

"But you're already friends with Kent," Bryn pointed out. "You've known him for years."

"Yeah. That's the problem. Kent just thinks of me as a friend. I need to get through to him somehow."

"Which is exactly why the DG is here." Devon nodded. "We will help each other."

Devon looked at Cassidy, as if she was waiting to hear about her main crush. But Cassidy wasn't ready to reveal this yet. She decided to delay the inevitable by putting the spotlight on someone else. "How about you, Bryn?"

Bryn's mouth twisted to one side like she was pondering something. "Well . . . I've always kind of wanted to get to know Jason Levine better."

Abby's brows arched. "Wow, you're setting your sights pretty high there, girlfriend."

Bryn shrugged. "Why not?"

Everyone knew that Jason was considered by many to

be the "golden boy" of Northwood. A senior, he was great looking, popular, athletic, class president, and an all-around good guy. As far as Cassidy knew, no one *didn't* like Jason.

"Yeah," Devon said. "Why not? I've seen him around. He's easy on the eyes and seems nice. Why shouldn't Bryn go for him? He's not taken, is he?"

"Jason used to date Amanda Norton," Abby told her. "She's a senior too. But according to gossip, Amanda was the one who broke up with him, and that was back in the summer."

"I never heard why they broke up," Bryn explained. "But I heard one of Amanda's friends acting like Amanda outgrew Jason."

"That's ridiculous," Devon said. "Probably just sour grapes."

"Except that I heard she's dating a college guy," Abby told her.

"So why shouldn't I go after him?" Bryn glanced at Devon like she was looking for backup. "I mean, I realize these are just the Dating Games and some of you might be willing to settle. But, hey, what if I go for it big-time? Is there a problem with that?"

Devon smiled. "I don't see why." She turned to Cassidy. "How about you? Who's your dream dude?"

Cassidy felt heat rising up her neck. This was something she'd never told anyone . . . something she'd never wanted anyone to guess. Now they were encouraging her to open up and lay her heart on the table in front of them—just like that? Could she even trust them?

"I know who it is," Emma said quietly.

Cassidy narrowed her eyes. "I don't think so."

Emma nodded a bit smugly.

"Who?" The other girls pressed Emma.

"Can I tell them?" Emma asked Cassidy.

Cassidy shrugged. Had she let this slip out to Emma? It seemed unlikely—although there was a time when she'd felt Emma was a safe confidante. Now she wasn't so sure.

"Fine," she told Emma in a slightly snippy tone. "Go ahead if you want, but I'll bet you don't even know which guy I'm thinking of."

Emma tilted her head to the side with a twinkle in her pale blue eyes. "It's Lane Granger."

Cassidy attempted not to appear shocked or fall out of her chair. Instead she looked down at her mocha as if it was thoroughly fascinating. How did Emma know this?

"Lane Granger?" Bryn said with a mix of surprise and admiration in her voice. "Who would've guessed?"

"I know Lane pretty well," Emma said. "In fact, he could become my first Dating Games project."

Cassidy frowned with concern.

"I mean, if it's okay with you." Emma looked uneasy. "I've known Lane since grade school. We have chemistry together this year. He talks to me."

"I think that's a brilliant idea," Devon told her. "Just remember the DG rules. You're going after him for Cassidy. No one else."

Emma nodded. "Absolutely."

Abby pointed at Bryn. "Didn't you used to be pretty good friends with Harris?"

"My Harris?" Devon's eyes lit up.

"Harris Martin," Bryn said quietly.

"Don't you guys still talk sometimes?" Abby asked Bryn. "I mean, I've seen you . . . right?"

Bryn shrugged like she was unsure or uncomfortable. Cassidy could tell that she felt cornered.

"How about it?" Devon pressed hopefully. "As a member of the DG, can you work on Harris for me?"

Bryn's blue eyes flickered with uncertainty, but she nodded. "Yeah . . . I guess so."

Devon frowned. "That's not very convincing. I mean, seriously, are you in this or not, Bryn? If you want out of the club, you can just say—"

"No. I'm in it," Bryn insisted.

"Then you should help Devon with Harris," Abby insisted, but then she smirked at Bryn. "That is, unless you want him for yourself." She elbowed Bryn. "Do you?"

Bryn looked embarrassed now. "No, of course not. I'll talk to Harris for you," she assured Devon. "I promise, I will. As soon as possible."

"Well, then." Devon smiled. "Like I said, *let the games begin.*"

Cassidy suspected that the games had already begun. She also suspected that the wise choice would be to bow out from this crazy excuse for a club. But it was like she couldn't somehow. Like her feet were glued to the floor. Maybe it was similar to watching a train wreck (or participating in one), but for some unexplainable reason—whose name began with *L*—she just wasn't ready to miss out on this.

4

Emma knew that she and Devon made a strange pair. Where Devon was flashy, Emma was frowzy. Where Devon had curves, Emma had bumps. But their moms had been best friends since their college days, and Emma and Devon had been friends since diapers. Somehow, despite their being in different schools the past few years, the friendship had stuck. But sometimes, like today, the oddity of their friendship caught Emma off guard.

"Maybe you should just give up on me," Emma told Devon as they sat together in Emma's room. Devon had been trying to talk Emma into changing her appearance—again. Like it was even possible. Devon's last-ditch effort, it seemed, was forcing Emma to stare at herself in the mirror. That wasn't helping. If anything, it only made Emma feel worse. "It's hopeless," she declared.

"It's not hopeless. I refuse to give up on my best friend," Devon said stubbornly. "Let's focus on your strengths."

Emma obediently remained in front of the full-length mirror, the mirror she normally avoided. How was she supposed to do an inventory of her dowdy appearance when all she could see was stringy dishwater-blonde hair that needed a wash, pale skin with a couple of random zits that never seemed to go away, faded blue eyes, a nondescript mouth, and a straight nose which was probably her best facial feature? "Not much to work with from the shoulders up." Her eyes moved reluctantly down. Although her faded sweatshirt concealed her lack of curves, she knew that her body had even less potential. "Really, Devon, I should just drop out of the DG," she said dismally.

"Why?"

"Because having me in it is going to mess it up for the rest of you."

"How's that?" Devon gathered Emma's hair, holding it up loosely as if she were trying to imagine it shorter. Like that would help. It had taken Emma two years to get her hair this long—barely past her shoulders. Her hair, similar to the fingernails she chewed, did not grow fast. But not because she chewed on it—thank goodness!

"You know," Emma continued, "because of the *no girl left behind* thing. Having me in the DG will ruin it for everyone else. Eventually you'll all hate me for slowing you down. So why don't I just quit now, before it's too late?" She pulled her hair out of Devon's hand, letting it fall loosely on her shoulders. She felt like crying but didn't want to look like a big baby.

"No way." Devon stood next to Emma now, frowning at the mirror with a finger on her chin like she was thinking hard. "You're one of the main reasons I wanted to create the DG in the first place."

Emma turned to peer at Devon. "Why?"

Devon smiled. "Because you're such a great person, Em. You are the sweetest person I know. But most people can't tell that by looking at you. It's not like you put any energy into your looks."

"What's the point?"

"The point is, you're sending a message."

"What's that?"

"That you don't have much self-worth."

"Maybe I don't base my self-worth on my looks," Emma said. "I know I'm smart, and I have a few talents. I'm a good artist. I'm just not a beauty queen. I never will be. Besides that, it's not healthy to obsess over your appearance."

"I know that. But completely neglecting yourself isn't healthy either." Devon sighed. "I know there are guys out there who would really like you—if they could get to know you. Seriously, Em, lots of guys would totally get you and appreciate you. But you'll never give them the chance, will you?"

"What difference does it make?" Emma felt her resolve to remain strong weakening.

"You'll never know if you don't try."

Emma shrugged. "Why bother? I mean, God made me the way I am. I can't complain about that, can I? What really matters is what's on the inside, right?"

Devon turned Emma around to face the mirror again. "Be honest, Em. You don't like your looks, do you?"

Emma still wanted to make a point. "Beauty is only skin deep," she told Devon. "God wants us to love and accept ourselves as we are."

Devon rolled her eyes like she wasn't buying this.

"Okay, I know you're not really a Christian anymore."

Emma was speaking carefully now. "I mean, you've made that clear. But I thought you used to be a Christian . . . back when you and your parents went to church."

"I only went to church because Dad made us. But after he left Mom, we quit going altogether. And to be honest, I don't miss it at all. I'm not saying you're a hypocrite, Em. But my dad is. A lot of other people are too. I just don't need that kind of falseness in my life."

Emma pressed her lips together. She already knew this. She and Devon had had this conversation numerous times over the past year—and it disturbed Emma and made her question their friendship. In fact, lately Emma was starting to think the only thing they really had in common was that both of them had been pretty much abandoned by their dads. Well, *abandoned* was probably too strong . . . but it felt like that sometimes.

"I'm sorry." Devon sighed. "I didn't mean to go into that again. I know you don't like it when I get on my anti-Christian soapbox."

"It's okay. Just so you know, though, I'm still praying for you. So I guess that makes us even."

Devon laughed. "Now back to the problem at hand. You never answered my question."

"What question?"

"Do you *like* your looks? And don't start preaching about how this is the way God made you because I'm not buying it. I mean, just because I'm not calling myself a Christian or going to church doesn't mean I quit believing in God altogether. And sure, God made us a certain way, but that doesn't mean he doesn't expect us to better ourselves. Like my mom wasn't born with glasses, but she can't see without them."

"That's different."

"I don't know." Devon frowned. "What about my cousin Bernice? She was born with a cleft palate. That was how God made her, right? But her parents didn't just let her stay like that. They paid thousands of dollars to get her mouth fixed. Do you think that was wrong?"

"No, of course not."

"So why can't we do a few *little* things to improve your appearance?"

Emma pressed her lips together.

"Why not?" Devon pressed. "Give me one good reason."

"Because it's useless." Emma walked away from the mirror, flopping onto her bed with a discouraged groan. "Remember, you tried it once. It didn't work. I ended up looking like a total freak."

Devon started laughing. "Oh, Em, you can't hold that against me. I was only thirteen and I'd just gotten that makeup kit for Christmas. I didn't know what I was doing."

"Yeah, and you painted me up and let me go to youth group looking like a hooker clown, and everyone made fun of me. I thought I'd never live that one down. You want to do it again?"

"That was a long time ago and you know it. You're just using it as an excuse. And it's a totally lame one."

Emma sat up and looked at Devon. The truth was, Devon had come a long way since then. She seemed to have figured out how to make the most of her own appearance. Of course, she had something to work with. Her hair color alone was stunning. In fact, Emma remembered a time when it had been more brown than red. "Do you do something to make your hair that color?" she asked Devon.

Devon reached up and patted her hair. "This marvelous auburn shade?" She giggled. "You don't think it's natural?"

"Well, it didn't used to have that much red in it. But it does look natural. Did it just change as you got older?" Emma frowned. "Mine did. It used to be more blonde, remember?"

"I do remember." Devon made a devilish grin as she checked out her own image in the mirror. "As a matter of fact, I do help my hair color out—just a little bit. My aunt introduced me to a hair product that's easy to use. Just a rinse that's also a conditioner. I put it on about every three to four weeks. Don't you think it looks nice?"

Emma nodded. "And natural. I can't believe I just figured out that it wasn't real." Suddenly she thought perhaps she was foolish not to trust Devon.

"So are you ready to put yourself in my hands?" Devon asked.

"I guess so. As long as you promise not to completely humiliate me again. And you need to understand that I don't have a lot of money to spend on this," Emma admitted. "I can't ask Mom. She's barely making it as it is."

"I already told you, it doesn't have to take much money. My aunt still does hair sometimes. Since her license is expired she can't even accept pay for it. She just does it for the fun of it sometimes. As long as you can cover the cost of the hair products, which shouldn't be too expensive, I'm sure we can come up with something cool for you."

"Do you honestly think she can help me?" Emma ran her fingers through her fine hair.

"I'm sure of it." Devon's brown eyes glimmered as she held up her cell phone. "Want me to call her right now?"

Emma let out a groan. Why was she letting Devon bully

her into this? And yet . . . why not? "Sure," she said without enthusiasm. "Knock yourself out."

Emma stared at the light on her ceiling as Devon talked to her aunt. Hopefully her aunt would be too busy. She had several small kids. How could she possibly have time to do something like—

"She said to come over around 1:00," Devon announced triumphantly.

"Seriously?" Emma sat up.

Devon nodded. "I promised to watch her kids for her while she works on your hair. She said we need to go to this hair supply place that her friend runs. She's going to call and tell her friend what we need to pick up."

"How does she know what I want?"

"I already told her."

"I heard you, Devon." Emma frowned. "You didn't say one word about my hair or what I—"

"I told her *before*." Devon was pressing numbers on her phone again. "Remember when I tried to get you to do this before school started?"

"Oh . . . yeah."

Devon talked to her mom on the phone, asking if she could use the car to go to her aunt Amy's house for the afternoon. Finally she closed her phone and grabbed Emma by the hand, pulling her up. "Get your purse," she told her. "Amy said the stuff we need to get should be about twenty dollars, and that's a bargain."

Emma started to question this, but Devon was already out in the family room, telling Emma's mom about the makeover plan. "Don't you agree that Em really needs it?" Devon said

45

to her in a conspiratorial tone. "I've been trying to get her to do this for ages."

Emma's mom smiled like she was amused. But then she always seemed to be amused by Devon's antics. "I already think Emma's a pretty girl, but I can't wait to see the results," she told them both.

"Can Em spend the night at my house?" Devon asked. "Please?"

Before Emma could protest—not that she particularly wanted to, except that she didn't like Devon bossing her around so much—Mom agreed. "But don't forget we're going to Grandma and Grandpa's for dinner tomorrow after church."

"Great." Devon turned back to Emma. "That way we can finish your makeover at my house."

"Just don't be late for church in the morning," Mom warned. "Are you coming too, Devon?"

Devon made a plastic smile. "I don't know for sure, but I promise to think about it."

"Good." Mom nodded, oblivious to Devon's insincerity. "How's your mom doing?"

"Okay. She's still getting used to her new job."

"Well, tell her hi for me—and that we need to get together soon. Maybe we can do lunch next week."

"Sure," Devon said. "I'll let her know."

Emma grabbed a few things and they were on their way. As they walked, she wondered how many times she'd made this short trek back and forth to Devon's house. She could probably find her way there blindfolded. Go four blocks down Simpson, turn right, cross the street, three more blocks, and there you are. The Fremonts' two-story brick house used to be in better shape, back before Devon's dad lost all interest in being a family man. The white trim paint was starting to peel. Lately Emma had also noticed that their yard, which used to be one of the nicest in the neighborhood, had started looking a little raggedy and sad.

But things at Emma's house had become run-down too. That was what happened when parents split. Her mom was so busy trying to keep everything together that it was only natural that some chores went undone. Grandpa used to do repairs before he started having health problems last year. Emma's brother, Edward, used to do yard work, but then he got a summer job, and now he was off at college. Emma did what she could to help occasionally, but most of the time it seemed like a losing battle. Why bother?

As the friends walked in the autumn sunshine, Devon chattered cheerfully about Emma's makeover. She was so enthused that Emma wasn't sure whether to be offended or worried. But Devon seemed to have it all mapped out—from head to toe. She'd obviously been planning this ambush for ages.

"After Amy finishes with your hair, we'll go back to my house and we'll both try out this new facial recipe that I found online. It's all natural. You mix yogurt and honey and oatmeal and just slather it on. Then we'll do manicures, and I'll work on your eyebrows, and by tomorrow you'll be a totally new woman."

Emma laughed nervously. "Yeah . . . right." But as they went into Devon's house, Emma decided that this attention was kind of nice. Hopefully Devon wouldn't be too disappointed when it was all said and done. Because Emma knew better than to expect much. Life had taught her that long ago.

•••••

"One of the only perks from my parents' divorce is the way Mom lets me use the car so much," Devon told Emma as she drove them over to her aunt's house. "Before the split, I didn't think I'd ever get to drive. But now it's like my mom doesn't really care."

"She cares," Emma assured her. "It's just that she's pretty laid-back." Emma tried not to feel jealous that Mrs. Banks rarely said no to Devon.

"I guess. Although I thought the divorce might've changed that—especially when she decided I had to switch schools. But last night I heard her on the phone fighting with Dad over money, and it made me think she moved me to Northwood just so she could stick it to him with my tuition."

"Well, I'm glad you're there," Emma told her. "You're lucky your mom's so easygoing. My parents' split turned my mom into a paranoid freak."

"She just loves you," Devon said.

Emma wasn't so sure. Sometimes it felt more like fear than love, and it had gotten even worse after Edward left for college. Mom was so overprotective that Emma sometimes felt like she was suffocating. And although Emma liked going to church, it was like her mom had become an addict. Whenever the doors were open, Emma's mom was there. Fortunately, she didn't insist that Emma do the same. As long as Emma made it to a Sunday service and an occasional youth group meeting, Mom was pacified. But if she had any idea of what Devon was really like (slightly boy crazy) or what kind of "influence" she brought (including this new Dating Games club) she wouldn't be nearly so supportive of their friendship. Not that Emma planned to tell her.

"I wish your mom could convince my mom to lighten up," Emma said wistfully as Devon parked in front of her aunt's house.

"Lighten up how?" Devon grabbed the mysterious bag that they'd picked up at the beauty supply store a few minutes ago.

"Like with dating. I can't even imagine what Mom would say if she knew I was planning to start dating." Emma rolled her eyes. "Like that's even going to happen. I mean, Isaac McKinley doesn't know I exist."

"It *is* going to happen," Devon said confidently. "You'll see."

"Even if Isaac was interested, I'd still have my mom to deal with."

"I'll talk to my mom," Devon promised as she rang the doorbell. "She'll get your mom to see that she needs to let go some."

"Devon." Amy opened the door with a relieved look. "Your cousins are in the family room. I promised you'd take them to the park." She pointed at Emma. "You, my dear, can head straight for the kitchen." She took the bag from Devon, and the next thing Emma knew, she was getting her hair washed in the kitchen sink.

"Oh, Emma, I've been wanting to get my hands on your hair for a long time," Amy said as she towel-dried Emma's shoulder-length hair. She peered down into Emma's face. "Can you trust me?"

Emma shrugged. "I don't know. I hope so."

"The style I have in mind is short, but it will be easy to keep up," Amy told her as she combed through the damp hair. "The color will make you look bright and fresh."

"Really?" Emma still felt uneasy.

"I promise. You're going to love it."

"What if I don't?" Emma reached up to touch her hair. "It's taken me so long to grow it."

"That's the problem, Emma. Some people should just give up on long hair. You're one of them."

"But what if I don't like short hair?"

Amy laughed as she snipped. "We'll get you some hair extensions."

Emma swallowed hard. There was no backing out now.

"I'm just going to cut off the length first," Amy explained. "Then I'll do the highlights. After that I'll cut your hair into a killer style."

Emma knew it was silly to feel like this, but tears filled her eyes as she watched strands of dishwater blonde hair falling to the kitchen floor. It had taken so long to grow her hair, and now this. Why had she agreed?

Emma kept her worries to herself, sitting quietly while Amy chattered and worked. "It's so nice to have a break from the kids," she said as she wrapped pieces of hair in foil. "I love doing hair. Although I'm not sure I'm ready to return to the salon yet. I want Benji to start preschool first."

Emma tried to at least appear to be listening, but all she could think about was that she was going to look like a boy when Amy finished. Flat chest and short hair—what a combination. She might as well kiss the DG good-bye too, because why would Isaac want to go out with a girl who looked like a boy?

A couple hours later, Amy announced that she was finished. "Let's go in the bathroom so you can see yourself." She reached for Emma's hand. "Come on, sweetheart."

Reluctantly, Emma let Amy lead her to the bathroom, and

after the lights were turned on, she braced herself to look into the mirror. In surprise, she reached up to touch the feathered layers of shimmering golden hair that framed her face. She looked completely different. Like someone else—and even slightly glamorous.

"You're gorgeous," Amy proclaimed.

Emma leaned forward, peering more closely. "I don't look like me."

"You look like a new and improved you," Amy said. "See how those highlights make your eyes sparkle? And that wispy cut is perfect for your heart-shaped face. You look absolutely adorable, Emma."

Emma turned and looked at Amy now. With her flushed cheeks and her dark hair pulled back in a tight ponytail, she looked slightly tired. "Thank you so much!" Emma hugged her. "I know that Devon is watching your kids so that you could do this for me, but I want to offer to babysit for you myself, as my own personal thank-you. You just name the time and day and I'll be here."

Amy blinked, then nodded eagerly. "That's an offer I won't refuse."

Just then Devon and the kids returned, and the house got noisy and crazy, with everyone crowding into the bathroom to see Emma's new haircut.

"It's so perfect." Devon ran her fingers through Emma's short hair. "You look like a fairy princess." She turned to Amy. "Nice work!"

Emma thanked Amy again as Devon insisted it was time to go home and continue with their makeover. This time Emma made no protests. Oh, she had no illusions. Even if Devon worked more magic with facials and makeup, there was nothing she could do about Emma's boyish figure. As Devon drove them back to her house, Emma got quiet. She knew that curvy figures were what usually caught the attention of high school boys.

"Do you honestly think this makeover will make any difference with Isaac?" Emma started feeling hopeless again as they went into Devon's house. It was one thing to change her hair, but as she looked down at her usual uniform of old jeans, a T-shirt, and Converse tennis shoes, she wondered how they could ever transform her into anything even slightly eye-catching.

"Are you kidding?"

"Look at me." Emma paused at the foot of the stairs, waving her hand down her torso. "I'm not exactly a femme fatale, if you know what I mean."

Devon laughed, slapping Emma on the back. "That's what I love about you, Em. So down to earth. Anyway, we're not done with you yet."

"But what if it's all for nothing?"

"Don't worry," Devon assured her. "Getting Isaac's attention isn't dependent on this makeover alone. I think it'll be a pretty good start, but I plan to work on him too."

Emma blinked. "You're going to work on Isaac?"

"Don't worry." Devon led the way into her room. "I will work very gently. So gently he won't even know what hit him."

Emma felt nervous now. Devon was a fun girl, but she was not known for being gentle or subtle. If anything, Devon was outspoken and risky. What if she messed this up for Emma? After all, Isaac was an intelligent guy. What if he saw right through Devon's matchmaking tactics? For that matter, what if he saw through Emma too?

Bryn was somewhat surprised to see that the call coming in on her cell was from Devon Fremont. It wasn't like Devon didn't know her number, but until yesterday's idea for the Dating Games, Bryn had never had much of a conversation with her. And despite what seemed like Devon's recent attempt to take over their little clique, Bryn still thought of Devon as the "new girl" and was slightly suspicious. At the same time, though, Bryn was curious. "Hey, Devon, what's up?"

"I need your help," Devon told her. "With a little project." She giggled like this was a joke.

"What kind of project?" Bryn pushed her computer aside. She was supposed to be working on a research paper but had gotten distracted by some impromptu online shoe shopping instead. Bryn wished she hadn't become such a slave to fashion this past year, but sometimes she just couldn't help herself.

"Well, I'm giving Emma a makeover, and—"

"A *makeover*?" Bryn shut her laptop. "For Emma?"

"Yeah, you should see her."

"That sounds like fun."

"So far it's going pretty good too. I mean, the hair and the makeup is a huge improvement. But to be honest, I'm kind of stuck when it comes to clothes." Devon let out a frustrated sigh. "We're on a pretty tight budget, and nothing in my closet is even close to working for her, and—"

"You need my help," Bryn filled in.

"Well, you always seem really fashionable. And Emma was just saying how she likes your style."

"Better than yours." Emma's voice came from the background.

"See, this is the thanks I get," Devon said. "Emma doesn't like any of the clothes I've been trying on her."

"They're too flashy for me," Emma called out in a pleading tone. "I'm not like that."

"Anyway, I thought you might have some ideas."

Bryn was already standing in front of her own closet. As usual, it was packed so full that it looked like it was about to explode. "Well, Emma's a little smaller than me," Bryn mused as she pulled out a Gap blouse that was too tight across the bust. "Especially in certain places." Bryn held the shirt up to herself and sighed. It had been so cute back when it fit properly. "I might have a thing or two that would work for her." Bryn tossed the shirt onto her bed. "That is, if you're serious. Emma isn't exactly a fashionista, if you know what I mean."

"She's changing her frumpy ways," Devon assured her. "You should see her now. Besides, if the DG is going to succeed, we need all the members to look hot. Remember?"

"That's true." Bryn surveyed her own image in the mirror on her closet door. Standing straighter, she flipped a section of long, blonde hair over a shoulder. It hadn't been that long since she'd felt like the ugly duckling. But the horrid braces had come off last year, her skin had cleared up last spring, and not long after she started working out every day, her figure had improved. It was only this past summer, for the first time since about fifth grade, that she actually began to feel pretty good about herself. Even though she hadn't been asked out yet, she could tell that some of the guys were noticing her this year. And if the DG worked, it should be only a matter of time before she was dating.

"Do you want to help us or not?" Devon asked.

Bryn reached for another shirt and then a sweater. "Sure. My closet is overdue for a thinning anyway. You guys want to come over here or what?"

After a brief discussion, it was agreed they'd come to her house. In the meantime, Bryn decided to start piling up any pieces that were too small for her. By the time Devon and Emma arrived, the mound on her bed was cascading onto the floor.

"Emma!" Bryn walked around Emma, checking out her new hairstyle. "You look fabulous." She touched the feathered layers of hair. "Very chic."

Emma's fine brows arched. "You think so?"

"Yes." Bryn nodded. Then she grimly shook her head. "Well, almost." She pointed to Emma's old blue sweatshirt and dumpy jeans. "From the neck down, we still have our work cut out for us."

"Which is why we're here," Devon reminded her.

Bryn pointed to the messy mound on her bed. "Have at it," she told Emma. "Everything there has got to go anyway."

"Seriously?" Emma's blue eyes got big.

"Absolutely." Bryn studied Emma more closely now. "It's amazing, Emma. You really do look different."

"Different good or different bad?" Emma frowned.

"Different as in fabulous. Like I said. But I have to admit there's something I'm not sure about." Bryn scrutinized Emma's face. The lip gloss seemed a little dark and the eye shadow a little intense. "I don't think I've ever seen you with that much makeup before. I'm not sure . . ."

Emma's hand went up to her cheek. "Is it too much, do you think?"

"Hey, wait a minute," Devon said. "I think she looks fine. Hot, even."

Bryn twisted her mouth to one side. "I'm not sure. I think it looks like she's trying too hard. She's got soft looks. Why not play those up?"

"See." Emma pointed at Devon. "I told you it was too much."

"You're just not used to it," Devon argued.

"I don't know." Bryn frowned. "To be perfectly honest, I think we should try to soften it up a little . . . you know, a more natural look."

Devon looked dubious, or else, more likely, she was offended, although Bryn had been trying to be as tactful as possible. Why was Devon so territorial when it came to Emma? Didn't she want her to look her best?

"I mean, you did a great job with her," Bryn reassured Devon. "Maybe you were doing her up the way you do your own makeup. With your auburn hair and striking coloring, it works. You can totally pull off those stronger colors. But Emma's a blonde . . . and not so dramatic. To be honest, I think she needs a more natural look."

Emma nodded eagerly. "I do. I do."

Devon seemed to consider this and finally just shrugged. "Yeah, you might be right."

"Anyway, let's look at the clothes for now," Bryn told them. "Start going through the pile and see if there's anything you can use. Try them on if you want."

But when Emma peeled off her sweatshirt and T-shirt to try on a Banana Republic sweater, Bryn couldn't help but laugh.

"What's so funny?" Emma asked defensively.

Bryn pointed to her bra. "That!"

Emma looked down at her chest and frowned.

"Sorry," Bryn told her. "It's just that's such a pathetic excuse for a bra. Why are you wearing *that*?"

Emma grabbed her sweatshirt and held it up like a shield, trying to hide the plain white sports bra. "My mom got these for me," she said meekly. "They were for volleyball, but they're actually pretty comfortable, and the straps don't slip around. I, uh, I have a bunch of them."

"Well, you should toss all of them," Bryn said abruptly. "Or else just use them for volleyball—and only if you don't care what you look like."

Emma scowled.

"Those bras make you look flatter than a pancake," Bryn explained. "Seriously, Emma. You need to go bra shopping. Without your mom."

Emma looked totally humiliated as she pulled her shirt back on.

"I'm sorry," Bryn said quickly. "Me and my big mouth."

"But Bryn's right," Devon told Emma. "That hideous bra is worse than useless."

Emma looked up with angry eyes. "What difference does

it make what kind of bra I wear?" she demanded. "I don't even *need* a bra. Sure, it's easy for you to make fun of me, but you have no idea what it feels like to be—"

"Hey, it wasn't that long ago that I looked exactly like you," Bryn told her. She got an idea. "I'll bet I have some bras that will fit you too." She hurried over to her dresser and pulled open her underwear drawer, pawing through it and digging deep until she found several double-A bras in various colors. "Here we go." She thrust them toward Emma. "That pink is from Victoria's Secret too."

"They're pretty," Emma admitted. "But they won't fit me."

"Just try them," Bryn urged.

Emma shook her head stubbornly. "It's pointless."

"Come on," Bryn encouraged her. "You can at least try."

"That's right," Devon said. "Go to the bathroom if you need the privacy, Emma. But at least try on the bras before you write them off."

Emma reluctantly took the bras, and after the bathroom door closed, Devon started giggling.

"It's not really funny," Bryn told her. "I mean, I remember feeling just like Emma does."

"But look at you," Devon said. "You're gorgeous."

While Emma tried on the bras, Bryn told Devon about how she used to look. To prove her point, she opened her laptop and pulled up some photos from the past couple of years.

"Oh, wow." Devon looked genuinely shocked. "I thought you were just born beautiful."

Bryn laughed. "My dad would be happy to tell you how much the braces cost. And that's just part of it."

"Well, it's nice that you're willing to help Emma like this. And don't forget that helping Emma is like helping the DG."

"Oh, yeah." Bryn had nearly forgotten the DG.

"By the way, have you had any luck with Harris?"

Bryn bit her lip. She'd also forgotten her promise to work on Harris for Devon. "Not yet," she assured her. "But it's barely been a day since we started the club. You can't expect something like this to happen overnight." Of course, now Bryn realized that she might've run into Harris at youth group tonight if she'd gone. He wasn't always there, but sometimes. She was about to ask Devon if she'd ever be interested in going with her, but now Emma was back.

She still had on her T-shirt, but it was obvious by the shape of it that she was wearing one of Bryn's old bras underneath.

"Look at you," Bryn told her.

"They fit!" she exclaimed happily. "I mean, they actually fit—as in I'm filling them up. It's not just air." She held her chest out, strutting around the room. "Look at me." She laughed. "I have *real* boobs."

"You just needed a real bra to go with them," Devon told her.

"Now you can try on some of these clothes," Bryn said.

It was unexpectedly fun seeing Emma trying on Bryn's old clothes. Emma was thrilled each time something fit or looked exceptionally good. Who knew anyone could be so jazzed to be given castoffs? Bryn wondered why she hadn't done something like this a long time ago. It was almost as good as shopping.

"You really, truly don't want these?" Emma asked Bryn for the umpteenth time as she hugged a bunch of clothes to her. "Honest to goodness?"

"Like I said, they're too small now," Bryn told her. "Some of those tops are from my freshman year. I mean, they're still cute and everything. They just don't fit right. They're all yours." Bryn went over to her closet, waving her hand like a game show host. "Now I have room in here for what actually fits."

"And room to buy more clothes," Devon teased.

Bryn gave them a sheepish grin. "My dad says I need a twelve-step program for shopaholics. But really, it's my only true vice."

By the time they had all of Emma's "new" clothes bagged up, it was nearly 8:00. "You guys could spend the night here if you want," Bryn offered hopefully. The idea had just occurred to her, but it sounded like fun.

"Thanks, but we still have some makeover stuff to work on at my house," Devon explained.

Bryn nodded. "Oh, yeah, sure." She wished they'd invite her to go home with them, but she wasn't going to be lame and hint. "I've got homework to finish anyway."

"Thanks for your help." Devon picked up one of the bulging shopping bags.

"Yeah, thanks for everything!" Emma smiled happily. "I feel like I just won the clothes lottery."

"Hey, you helped me clean out my closet." Bryn picked up a T-shirt that had fallen out of Emma's bag and stuffed it back in. As she walked them to the front door, she wished there was a way to prolong their visit, but she knew it was too late. They were going. She stood by the window, watching as they got into the car and pulled out.

Bryn closed the blinds and sighed. She felt inexplicably lonely now. It was probably her fault since she had chosen not to go to youth group. That was because Abby was away with her family, and Bryn didn't like going alone. As usual for a Saturday night, her parents were at their small group meeting. The big house felt quiet and empty.

As she walked to her room, she thought about how it used to be. All the years she was growing up, her four older siblings had filled this place with noise and chaos and friends and constant activity. She had taken it for granted then. In fact, she sometimes had complained about it. But now that they were gone, either at college or jobs or just living their own lives, it was way too quiet . . . and sometimes it was a little depressing.

She thought about calling her best friend, except that she knew Abby was at a family wedding, probably at the reception by now. Even so, Bryn texted her to say she missed her but hoped she was having fun. Then she told her that Emma and Devon had been by, making it sound like more than it was. That was probably just loneliness talking. But Abby would understand.

Bryn opened her computer, but instead of doing homework, she went back to shoe shopping. As she was imagining how she'd look in a pair of leopard print Louboutins, she thought about Devon's question regarding Harris. She clicked over to Facebook to check out Harris's page.

No one knew about it—well, except maybe Abby, if she even remembered—but Bryn used to have a crush on Harris Martin. For years while she was nothing more than a youth group wallflower, she had watched Harris, wishing he'd suddenly look at her and see beyond her plain Jane exterior. Of course, it never happened.

At the beginning of this school year, though, thanks to her new and improved appearance, she had felt more hopeful than ever. However, she'd been caught off guard when

Devon announced that she planned to pursue Harris for herself. Bryn had considered arguing her own case with Devon but decided not to. Harris might not be interested in Devon anyway. Besides that, Harris's best friend, Jason Levine, had been unexpectedly friendly to Bryn recently.

Thanks to the DG, Bryn wanted to focus on capturing Jason's attention. He was an all-around nice guy and very good looking. What girl wouldn't be thrilled to go to the homecoming dance with him? But in her heart, she suspected she was only trying to snare Jason in the hopes of attracting Harris's attention. The old grass is greener theory. If Harris saw Jason with Bryn, he'd be jealous.

Oh, she knew it was far-fetched. Because really—whether it was due to Mr. Worthington's yearly guy talk or something else, neither of those boys seemed to be terribly interested in dating right now anyway. She doubted that the efforts of the DG were really going to change that. Still, it could be fun to try.

Studying the pictures on Harris's photo page, she wanted to make a comment on one of them. She'd never done this before, not with Harris anyway, but since she was on a mission for Devon's sake, she decided to throw caution to the wind. She went through all the photos and finally decided on a shot of both Harris and Jason together. Wearing only their swim trunks, suntans, and big grins, they appeared to be on a small boat and were holding up a strange-looking fish with a gigantic mouth.

"Pretty hot guys," she typed into the comment slot, "but not nearly as hot as that sea creature they're holding." She giggled as she hit Send. Okay, let the conversation begin.

A bby knew she was lucky. Okay, she was *blessed*—at least that's what her parents would say. They were always quick to remind her that although it wasn't always easy being black in a predominantly white school, she had a lot to be grateful for. For one thing, her parents were still happily married after more than twenty years now. Besides that, they both had solid careers—her dad was the dean at the local Christian college, and her mom taught sociology there. They attended church fairly regularly, and compared to some of Abby's friends' lives, her life was considered "stable" and "normal."

Even so, it wasn't always easy being an only child. Or being one of the few ethnic minority kids at Northwood. But Abby knew better than to complain to her parents about such things. They would only launch into a sad story about how it was when they were growing up. Worse yet, they'd go into a *P*s speech—reminding her of how her grandparents put up with prejudice and persecution and participated in peace marches and protests. She'd heard it a hundred times. It wasn't that she didn't appreciate black history. She absolutely did. But sometimes she just wanted to be like everyone else. Was that too much to ask?

To be fair, it was what her parents wanted too. At least they wanted her to be just like them. In their minds there was no higher aspiration. For the most part, Abby didn't disagree, but sometimes it seemed the only thing they talked about was her future: what college she would attend, what kind of scholarships to apply for, how she would contribute to society as an adult. Sometimes they were so focused on how her life was going to be someday that it seemed like they lost complete sight of the here and now.

For instance, as they were driving home from Aunt Rebecca's wedding tonight and she was reading texts from Bryn about their new club and how things were moving along, she felt left out of the fun—like life once again was passing her by. She wanted to be there with them to see Emma's makeover, and she wanted to start making some progress on the Dating Games plan. But at the same time, she was worried. What if her parents disapproved of the DG?

She'd never even broached the subject of dating with them before. Not because she'd been avoiding the topic, but more because it had never come up. She'd never been asked out before, and in all honesty, it seemed unlikely she'd be asked out now. Yet considering the progress Bryn seemed to be making, she felt slightly hopeful. But what if she got asked out and her parents said no?

As the car zipped down the interstate, she wondered if this might be the perfect time to introduce a new topic of conversation with her parents: dating and why they should let her do it. However, she knew timing was everything. Was this really the right time? She ran the pros and cons around in her mind, finally deciding that she had a captive audience. Not only were they stuck in the front seat for two more hours, but they were worn out from the past two days of wedding festivities.

"I want to talk to you about something," she began carefully.

"What?" Mom asked with not much interest.

"I've been thinking about something." She paused, trying to think of the right words. She'd been in debate club for a year now. She considered herself to be good at persuasive talking. "I'd like to get your opinion on it."

"What kind of something?" Dad sounded slightly suspicious, but he kept his gaze straight ahead, obviously focusing on the freeway traffic—a trail of red taillights for as far as she could see.

Mom turned around in the seat to peer curiously at her. "What are you thinking about, honey?"

"Well, it's occurred to me that I'll be seventeen in November, and I've never been on a real date."

Dad laughed, then answered in a sing-song way, "And that's the way, uh-huh-uh-huh, I like it. Uh-huh-uh-huh."

"Very funny." Abby rolled her eyes. "Anyway, some of my friends have been talking about going to the homecoming dance, and I thought maybe I'd like to go too."

"That's a nice idea." Mom nodded with an approving expression. "Is there a particular boy you think is going to ask you?"

"Wait a minute." Dad glanced at Mom, then back at the

road. "Are you saying she can go? Just like that? We don't even know this boy. And from what I've heard, high school dances are getting way out of hand these days."

"Dad," Abby said in exasperation. "This is Northwood Academy we're talking about. Nothing gets out of hand there."

"Well, you never know. For instance, your mom and I work at what is supposedly a good Christian college, and yet some of the things that have happened there—well, don't get me going."

"That's life, Bruce. Just because a few college kids make bad choices doesn't mean Abby is going to. Look how responsible she's been. And she keeps her grades up. I really don't see anything wrong with her going to a dance." Mom peered at Abby. "You mentioned your friends are going. Which ones?"

"And who's the boy?" Dad demanded.

"It's not for sure." Abby wished she hadn't started this conversation.

"Who is he?" Dad asked. "Is there some reason you don't want us to know his name?"

"Only because he hasn't even asked me," she said in frustration. "But if you must know, his name is Kent Renner. He's a really nice guy. He's a good musician, he's academic, and he plays basketball and soccer too."

"He sounds well-rounded and interesting," Mom said.

"Sure, he *sounds* great," Dad said doubtfully, "but that's from her perspective. We don't even know him."

"Will it be a group date?" Mom asked.

Abby wasn't really sure about the group date thing, but because she seemed to have Mom's support, she decided to just go with it. "I'm pretty sure it'll be a group date," she said quickly. "Bryn and Cassidy and Emma would go too."

"I like those girls." Mom nodded.

"And a new girl too."

"Who's that?" Dad asked, and again the suspicion crept into his voice. Abby knew it was because he loved her and because he had only one daughter to focus on. Just one more reason she wished she wasn't an only child.

"Her name's Devon Fremont," she told them. "She's been friends with Emma since they were babies. She just transferred to Northwood because her mom thought the public schools were losing their academic edge."

"That and a few other things too," Dad said. "From what I hear, anyway."

"Is Devon a nice girl?" Mom asked. It was funny how oblivious parents could be when they asked questions like that. How did they expect their kids to answer?

"Yeah. She's really nice. We've been trying to make her feel at home at Northwood. I can't imagine how hard it would be to switch schools like that."

"That's so kind of you." Mom smiled.

"So you guys are cool with me dating, then?" Abby asked hopefully. This was going even better than she had expected.

"I wouldn't go that far," Dad said a bit sharply.

"Oh, Bruce." Mom sighed. "We have to let her grow up someday. Like she said, she's almost seventeen. Remember what you were doing at her age?"

"Ugh. Don't remind me. That's precisely why I'd prefer she postpone dating for a while."

"Why?" Abby asked.

"Because I remember it well. I know what boys are like

at that age. *Seventeen*." He grimly shook his head. "Their testosterone is running rampant, and they're after one thing and one thing only."

Mom giggled. "Bruce, that's so judgmental."

"So, Dad, do you mean that's what you were like when you were seventeen?" Abby asked.

Dad cleared his throat. "Well, I, uh . . . no."

"Tell the truth," Mom urged.

"Well, sure, I had hormones like any other normal seventeen-year-old boy. But I also knew how to keep them under control. My parents taught me to respect girls." He chuckled. "My mama would've taken a belt to me if I didn't."

"Don't you think there are still some nice boys out there?" Mom said to him. "And don't you think we've raised our daughter to be aware of what makes for a nice boy . . . and how to recognize the other kind and go the best direction?"

Dad rubbed his chin. "Well, I'd like to think so. I certainly hope so."

Abby knew this was her chance. "You've always set a great example, Dad. I mean, I see how well you treat Mom and other women. Why would I settle for a guy who wasn't at least trying for those standards? You've set the bar pretty high, but at least it's something to aim for."

"Thank you, Abigail. I guess it's a little unfair to assume that all seventeen-year-old boys are after one thing only." Dad sighed. "I'm sure there must be some good young men out there. Especially at Northwood."

"Are you saying it's okay for me to date?"

"I suppose I'm opening up to the idea. Maybe we can see how it goes with one date—as long as it's a group date—and take it from there."

Abby was tempted to argue this point but realized that might ruin everything. "Sure, I think that would work."

"This is so exciting," Mom said with real enthusiasm. "Your first formal dance. Do you know what you want to wear yet?"

"Not really."

"How far out is the dance?"

"Three weeks."

"Oh, that gives us some time. But we should start shopping soon."

"Uh-huh . . ." Abby wasn't so sure she wanted to shop for her dress with her mom, but after making this much progress on the whole dating thing, and since Mom had been so solidly in her court, she didn't want to rock the boat. Still, the idea of Mom picking out her dress was a little unsettling. It wasn't that Mom had bad taste—for her age she dressed pretty fashionably—but Mom had picked out the dress Abby had been forced to wear to Rebecca's wedding, and although Abby wasn't actually in the wedding party, Mom had wanted to be sure she'd fit in for the photos. But Abby would never, never wear that awful pink ruffled dress again. Even now it was wadded into a ball and stuffed into her suitcase.

As Mom continued talking about dresses and corsages and dinners and all sorts of dance-related things, Abby tried to act like she was listening while she was texting Bryn, assuring her that everything was moving along smoothly on her end. This was so exciting!

Abby leaned back against the seat and sighed happily. She was thankful that the focus on dating and jerky guys had distracted her dad from asking more specifically about the guy she had in mind. Oh, she had an answer ready for him, but it was a relief not to be forced to use it. Not because it was a lie, because it wasn't. Abby might be comfortable using various tactics to work her parents—who didn't?—but she refused to flat-out lie to them.

She imagined how cool it was going to be to walk into the dance next to Kent Renner. She had been seriously crushing on the tall basketball player for more than a year now, ever since he transferred to their school. Of course, she'd known him before he came to Northwood. They'd gone to the same church for years, until her family had switched churches. After that, she'd naturally lost track of him.

She'd been thrilled to see him again when he'd started school at Northwood last year, and equally thrilled that he recognized her. It seemed they even had something of a friendship. Okay, *friendship* might be a stretch, or just her imagination. But at least Kent knew her name and spoke to her occasionally. She'd had several classes with him and was comfortable saying "Hey" to him now and then. Not too obsessively, since she didn't want to scare him off. As far as she could tell, Kent had never had a girlfriend. At least not since coming to Northwood. He was a senior, so this would be his last year in high school . . . his last homecoming dance . . . that alone should be reason enough to make him consider going. But how was she going to bring it up?

Then she remembered—that was what the DG was for. They were supposed to help each other. But at their meeting on Friday no one had offered to come to her assistance. Probably because Bryn had pointed out that Abby was already on good terms with Kent. That wasn't really fair, though. Just because they were friends didn't mean she could walk up and ask him to go to the dance. And if this club was going to work the way Devon had described, she shouldn't have to.

Abby considered her friends, wondering which one would be best to get the wheels rolling with Kent. Devon would probably say too much. Emma wouldn't say enough. Cassidy . . . well, she might end up giving him a lecture on morals and ethics. Finally Abby decided that it would probably have to be Bryn since she was Abby's best friend. Plus she knew Kent well enough to have a somewhat natural conversation with him.

With this in mind, she grabbed her phone again. Bryn had already texted her back, congratulating her on handling her parents. Abby texted again, asking Bryn to be the go-between with Kent. She even offered to help with Jason in exchange, if needed. However, as she hit Send, she doubted her assistance would be needed. Bryn was so pretty and smart and fun, Jason would probably leap at the chance to take her out. Especially since he wasn't with Amanda now. Really, of all the girls, Bryn had it made. It was simply that she didn't know it. For so many years Bryn had thought of herself as plain and ugly. Nothing could be further from the truth now. Not that Abby brought this up so much. Who wants their best friend to get a big head?

As she slipped her phone back into her bag, she thought about Kent some more. The first question her parents would want to ask her—but knowing them, they wouldn't—would have to do with his ethnicity. When she told them (and she would have to) that he was white, they would act like this was no big deal. After all, they were educated and open-minded. But she would see behind their eyes and know that they didn't completely approve.

At Aunt Rebecca's wedding last night, she'd overheard Mom talking quietly to an aunt. "Hopefully, the third time's the charm," Aunt Betty had said regarding Rebecca's third marriage. "Maybe this one's going to last."

"I hope so." Mom had frowned at the newlywed couple as they attempted an awkward version of salsa dancing for the crowd. "I just wish her taste hadn't gone so vanilla on us."

Aunt Betty had just shaken her head, as if she felt the same.

"But he does seem like a good man," Mom had said with quick remorse. "Naturally I wish them the very best."

Abby had no doubt that Mom wished her sister the very best. She also knew that Mom secretly wished that Aunt Rebecca had married a black man. However, Mom would probably never admit this to Abby. She would probably bite her tongue where Kent was concerned too. Even so, she would not be pleased to see Abby bringing home a white guy. Neither would Dad.

But what did they expect when they sent her to an almost all-white school? Northwood had just a handful of black students, including only two guys. One was a freshman. The other was a junior who was a jock and full of himself. He wasn't the type who attracted her, and from what she could tell, he felt the same about her. However, Kent had always caught her eye, and not just because he was good looking, although he was. He was also a really good guy.

She remembered the day when Kent had given her a sample of his true colors. She'd been heading to drama with an armload of costumes that she'd picked up at the cleaners. Hurrying too fast, her foot got tangled in the plastic, and she nearly fell flat on her face. In that same moment, Kent had reached out and caught her, saving her from pain and humiliation. She gazed into his bluer than blue eyes as he steadied her. Then he helped carry the bulky costumes all the way to the drama department. That was true chivalry.

Anyway, what difference did it make who she went to the dance with? It wasn't like she was going to marry her first date. But even if they did fall madly in love and eventually (like after college) decided to tie the knot, what would be wrong with that? She knew of lots of perfectly happy inter-racial couples. Why should anyone limit themselves to their own ethnic group? Wouldn't that make this world a totally boring place?

Devon was actually glad to go to school on Monday. Not only did her best friend look like a completely new person, but it felt like all the girls were excited about the DG. They'd been texting back and forth over the weekend, and it seemed that each girl wanted to do her part to make this club succeed. Well, except maybe for Cassidy. She sometimes seemed like she was dragging her heels.

"That's just the way she is," Emma told Devon as they walked toward school together. "She's kind of a worrywart, you know, a glass half empty instead of half full kind of girl. But I know she's really interested in Lane Granger, and since I'm willing to work on him for her, I'm guessing she'll do her part for the DG."

"Bryn texted me last night that she's been having a conversation with Harris on Facebook."

"For you?" Emma sounded concerned.

"Of course it's for me." Devon tried not to look offended. "Who else?"

Emma shrugged. "I don't know."

"Are you saying Bryn's not trustworthy?"

"No, of course not." Emma shook her head. "It's just that this is all kind of tricky. I mean, how do we keep track of which girl is working on which guy . . . for which girl?"

Devon laughed. "Well, I made a chart last night. I'll show it to the club at lunch. The only girl not actively working on a guy right now is Cassidy."

"Does that mean someone else is going to be left out?" Emma pushed open the door.

"No, because Bryn is actually working on two guys. Harris for me, and Kent for Abby. But it was her idea. She offered."

"So Cassidy is getting off easy."

"Not too easy." Devon smiled. "I have plans for her."

"Speaking of your plans," Emma said quietly. "You won't go overboard on Isaac, will you? I don't think he's the kind of guy you can push around, and I'm worried he'll know what you're up to and—"

"Emma." Devon stopped walking and turned to look into Emma's eyes. "Do you trust me or not?"

"I, uh, I'm not sure. I mean, yeah, I trust you. But you don't really know Isaac that well . . . and I'm worried he'll be suspicious and—"

"I know what I'm doing, Emma. Just trust me. Okay?"

Emma nodded, but she still looked uneasy.

"It's not like I'm going to twist his arm or threaten him within inches of his life," Devon told her as they went to their lockers. "Seriously, Em, he's not even going to know I'm working on him."

"If you say so," Emma mumbled.

Devon stopped in front of her locker, turning again to look at Emma. Why was she acting so paranoid now? "Look, Emma, you're my best friend. I won't sabotage this for you." She smiled. "Did you look at yourself in the mirror this morning?"

Emma barely nodded, glancing around in a nervous and self-conscious way.

"You look stunning. If I was going to sabotage you, would I have helped you to get that makeover?"

"No, that's not what I'm worried about."

"Then stop worrying." Devon poked her in the arm. "And stand up straight. Hold your head high. Don't go around acting like you still want to blend in with the walls. You look gorgeous now. Act like it."

Emma looked embarrassed now. "Really? Gorgeous?"

"You'll see." Devon shoved some books into her locker and closed it. "Come on, let's go see how the others react."

Soon they found Abby, and she was blown away by Emma's new look. "You are looking good," Abby told her. "Really hot."

Emma smiled. "Thanks."

"See." Devon waved over to Cassidy and Bryn, who were just coming into the locker bay.

"Wow—Emma." Cassidy was suitably impressed. "Look at you."

Emma stood a little taller now.

"What happened?" Cassidy asked.

"She had a little makeover," Devon told her. "Remember, we all agreed to do some self-improvement." She pointed at Cassidy. "You could use a little help too . . . if you know what I mean."

Cassidy frowned. "Huh?"

"No offense, but your look is a little . . . well . . . ho-hum."

The other girls giggled, and Devon could tell she'd offended Cassidy.

"I'm sorry," Devon said quickly. "I wasn't trying to hurt your feelings. But if you're going to catch Lane's eye, you might want to put a little more effort into it."

"We can help you," Bryn said hopefully.

"Sure." Abby nodded eagerly. "We'll start with your wardrobe."

"My clothes are fine," Cassidy snapped.

"Yes." Bryn wrinkled up her nose. "Hoodies are so fashionable."

"And so last, uh, century," Abby teased.

"Hoodies are always in style," Cassidy insisted as she pulled the navy sweatshirt more tightly around her.

"Come on," Devon urged. "You could try harder, couldn't you?"

"I don't know." Cassidy looked like she was pouting now.

"I was *going* to start working on Lane today," Emma interjected. "But maybe I should wait."

Cassidy suddenly seemed worried. "Yes. You should wait." She looked from Devon to Bryn and Abby. "Fine. I'll do some kind of makeover. Not a major one like Emma got. But I suppose you're right. I could probably use a little help."

"That's the spirit." Devon slapped her on the back. "Welcome to the club."

"I'll hold off on talking to Lane," Emma assured her.

"How am I supposed to pull off this makeover magic?" Cassidy asked. "Any suggestions?"

"Why don't you let us take you under our capable wings?" Bryn suggested with a sly smile. "Abby and me."

"Really? You'd do that?"

"Sure. If you let us. Do you trust us?"

With an uncertain expression, Cassidy nodded, and everyone seemed to agree this was a good plan. As Devon walked to her first class, she felt confident. Everything was under control, and she felt sure that everything was going to stay under control. Creating the DG had really turned out to be a great idea. She continued in this positive frame of mind until she emerged from her fourth period class and noticed a girl giggling with Harris Martin—her Harris.

She couldn't really see who the girl was because she was partially obscured by a post, but the two were standing noticeably close, as if they were a couple! This was news to Devon. The girl threw back her head, flipping a section of long, blonde hair over a shoulder as she leaned in closer. It seemed clear that this chick was putting the moves on Devon's dream guy, but what could she do?

Wanting a better look, and wishing she could put a stop to what was happening, Devon approached the couple. Of course, she knew there was nothing she could do, but at least she could assess the damage. As she got closer, a shock wave ran from her scalp to her toes—the flirtatious blonde was none other than Bryn Jacobs! Bryn, who was supposed to be working on Harris for Devon, was going after Harris for herself. She was breaking rule number six of the DG.

Furious, Devon wanted to approach and confront the pair. She wanted to give Bryn a fierce warning look and even say something snarky. But she knew that would ruin everything. Besides, she reminded herself, Bryn had offered to work on Harris for Devon. Maybe that was what she was doing.

Yeah, right, she thought as she stormed off in the other

direction. Bryn was working on Harris for herself. Not for Devon. That was what she got for trusting this task to the prettiest girl in the group. Naturally, it would backfire. Why hadn't Devon considered this? Devon decided to take the long route to the cafeteria. That would give her time to cool off some. But by the time she entered the dining area, she was seriously vexed, and she didn't care who knew it.

"Where's Bryn?" she growled at Abby.

Abby looked surprised. "I don't know. What's wrong?"

Devon slammed her bag down on a chair.

"What's going on?" Emma asked Devon with concern. "You look really upset."

Devon let out a seething breath. "Bryn was flirting with Harris."

The girls looked slightly shocked, and that in itself brought Devon a smidgeon of comfort. At least they could see that Bryn had crossed the line. Even so, Devon was still furious.

"You must be imagining things," Abby said defensively. "Bryn wouldn't do something like that."

"Well, she was doing it." Devon scowled. "I saw her."

"That doesn't sound like Bryn to me," Emma said quietly.

Devon turned to glare at Emma. Was this really her best friend?

"Bryn's not a backstabber," Abby said.

"You're sure about that?" Devon narrowed her eyes.

"Wasn't Bryn supposed to be working on Harris for *you*?" Cassidy asked her.

Devon nodded grimly. "Oh, yeah . . . she was working on him, all right."

"What happened to *innocent until proven guilty*?" Abby asked. "Bryn should get a chance to defend herself."

"There she is now." Cassidy pointed to where Bryn was entering the cafeteria, flanked by Harris and Isaac. All three were smiling and talking, and it seemed pretty clear to Devon that Bryn, who seemed to be in her element, was blatantly flirting.

"Look, she's even moving in on Isaac," Devon warned Emma. "Better keep your eye on that girl."

"Oh, I don't think—"

"I don't know why I ever trusted her."

"Devon." Emma sounded irritated. "Give her a break."

Devon watched as Bryn parted ways with the guys and, wearing a big smile like nothing was wrong, practically skipped over to their table. Devon was determined to keep her cool, or at least try to get it back, and tried to disguise the fact that she was seething.

"What's up?" Abby asked Bryn when she joined them.

"Yeah," Devon chimed in. *"What's up?"*

Bryn's smile faded. "What's wrong with you?"

Devon did a quick eye roll, then shrugged. "Nothing."

Bryn looked unconvinced.

"She's bent out of shape because she thinks you're trying to steal Harris," Abby informed her.

"Rule number six." Abby held up the little DG notebook she'd made over the weekend. "Never steal a fellow DG member's boyfriend."

"Harris isn't your boyfriend *yet*." Bryn's voice sounded a bit snippy.

"But that was the plan," Devon reminded her.

"That's true," Emma added.

"FYI"—Bryn scowled at Devon—"I was *not* trying to steal your boyfriend. I should say *future* boyfriend since it's not even established that he likes you."

"Then what were you doing?" Devon demanded.

"I was doing exactly what you asked me to do, Devon. I'm warming him up for you. Isn't that what you wanted?"

Devon shook her head. "He doesn't need that kind of warming." She held up her own notebook now. "Maybe we need to change our game plan."

"What's that?" Abby asked.

"Our official notebook," Devon explained. "I charted out which girl is working on which guy for which girl." She knew that sounded convoluted. "To avoid confusion . . . like we're having today."

"But you assigned Harris to me," Bryn pointed out.

"We didn't assign Isaac to you," Emma told her. "Seemed like you were warming him up too."

"Hey, he was there. And he's Harris's best friend. What am I supposed to do? Ignore him?"

"No . . . of course not." Emma looked flustered.

Devon felt like her blood pressure had gone down ever so slightly. "Let's get our lunches and meet back here to go over this again," she told them. "If this plan is going to work, we need to be on the same page."

By the time they reconvened at their table, Devon had calmed down. Perhaps she'd overreacted. After all, she had asked Bryn to break the ice with Harris. Of course, she didn't want Bryn to melt the boy down into a lukewarm puddle. But maybe Bryn couldn't help the effect she had on guys. Why was it that long-legged blondes always seemed to have the advantage?

"So tell us about your little book." Abby pointed to the nondescript-looking notebook.

Devon took a sip of water, then opened the book. The first

few pages were intentionally left blank, just in case someone picked it up, although Devon planned to keep it safe. Under lock and key if necessary. The first page with writing had the DG rules. She turned to the next page.

"I've assigned us secret names," she explained.

"Huh?" Cassidy leaned over to see.

"In case someone found this," Devon told her.

"Oh, yeah." Abby nodded. "Good plan."

"Our secret names begin with our first initial," she told them.

"What's mine?" Abby asked.

"You're Angel."

Abby laughed. "Oh, yeah, that suits me to a T."

"I'm Desiree," Devon said. "Cassidy is Candy. Bryn is Babe. And Emma is Ecstasy."

"Ecstasy?" Emma frowned. "That's a drug."

"It's also a word," Devon said.

"Those sound like hooker names," Cassidy declared.

"Or strippers," Abby added.

Emma peered down at the notebook. "Candy, Angel, Babe, Desiree, Ecstasy—are you kidding?"

"It's just a privacy tactic," Devon retorted. "Who would ever guess who we were based on those names?"

Bryn laughed. "Babe works for me."

Devon rolled her eyes. "Yeah, I figured."

"Whatever you say, *Desiree*." Bryn pointed her finger at Devon.

"We're not supposed to actually *use* these names on a daily basis," Devon explained. "They're only for certain situations. Like if we're texting about someone, or if you need to discreetly say something in front of someone."

"Do the guys have fake names too?" Emma asked.

"I thought I'd let you guys make up names for your special guys," Devon told them. "I already have one for Harris."

"What is it?" Abby asked.

"Hunk." Devon smirked. "It seems to suit him."

Bryn laughed. "Sure does."

Devon scowled at her.

"What can I call Kent?" Abby's brow creased. "What starts with *K*?"

"Killer," Cassidy suggested. They all laughed.

"I like it," Abby said. "Killer it is."

"Maybe you should call Lane *Lover Boy*," Devon told Cassidy.

Cassidy turned up her nose. "No way."

"I can't think of anything good that starts with an *I*," Emma said in frustration. "How about if I call him Newton?"

"Newton?" Bryn tipped her head to one side.

"You know," Emma said. "Like Sir Isaac Newton."

Bryn laughed. "Oh, yeah. All I could think of was *Fig Newton*."

"Maybe you should call him Fig," Devon suggested as she wrote down the code names. The other girls laughed.

"This is fun." Abby pointed at Bryn. "What are you calling Jason?"

"How about JT?"

"I guess that works," Devon said.

"But what's the *T* for?" Cassidy asked.

Bryn shrugged. "I don't know. It just sounded good. Maybe it's for Terrific." She poked Cassidy. "You better think of something for Lane before he becomes Lover Boy."

"Larry," Cassidy proclaimed.

"Larry?" Devon studied her. "That's kind of blah, don't you think?"

"Fine. Call him Larry the Tomato then."

"Larry the Tomato?" Devon was confused.

"You know, from VeggieTales," Cassidy told her.

"No, that was Larry the Cucumber," Abby corrected. "I know because I used to be addicted to those cartoons."

"Are you sure?" Cassidy looked skeptical. "I thought it was Larry the Tomato."

"How about just plain Larry," Devon said as she filled in the name and turned the page. "Now we need to go over our assignments so everyone is clear. I've rearranged a little, so listen closely." Devon studied her book, trying to remember the code names they'd just assigned to the guys. "Okay . . . Ecstasy is working on Larry for Candy." She paused to look at her friends, who looked slightly confused. "Do you get it or not?"

"Emma is working on Lane for Cassidy," Abby proclaimed.

They all nodded, agreeing that was correct.

"Go on," Bryn told Devon. "This is fun. Kind of like a game."

"It is a game," Devon reminded her. "Dating Games. Remember?"

"Yeah, yeah. Tell us the rest," Abby urged.

"Okay . . . Babe is working on Killer for Angel."

Cassidy actually laughed now. "This sounds like the description of some weird movie."

"As long as we don't flop at the box office, who cares?" Bryn said. "I'm working on Kent for Abby. But I'm also working on Hunk for Desiree, right?"

"Not anymore," Devon told her.

Bryn frowned. "Just because of—"

"No," Devon said quickly. "I'd already reassigned Harris—I mean Hunk—to, uh, Candy."

"Why?" Bryn looked disappointed.

"Because Cassidy didn't have an assignment. It seems only fair that we each have one guy to work on."

"I already started on Harris." Bryn stuck out her lower lip.

"Thanks," Cassidy told her. "I appreciate the help. But I'll take it from there."

Devon felt relieved—as well as surprised that Cassidy was playing along so well. She'd expected more heel-dragging.

"I mean, it's only fair. Everyone should do their share," Cassidy said.

"That's right," Devon told her. "And Angel is working on JT for Babe."

"We're supposed to remember all that?" Emma asked.

"I'll email you a list tonight," she said. "You can print it out and delete it."

"Like real spies," Emma said.

"Except that you can never fully delete anything from the internet," Abby pointed out.

"Which is precisely why we're using code names," Devon reminded them. She wrote something at the top of the page. "I'll call this the Hit List."

They laughed, and then the bell rang and they set off for their various classes. With a feeling of accomplishment, Devon slipped the notebook into her bag. By the end of the day, she'd sent the revised list as an email to the other members of the DG.

The Hit List

- Desiree works on Newton for Ecstasy
- Babe works on Killer for Angel
- Ecstasy works on Larry for Candy
- Candy works on Hunk for Desiree
- Angel works on JT for Babe

Devon couldn't help but laugh as she reread this strange message later that night. It really sounded pretty ridiculous. Still, she hoped it would provide some much needed clarity for everyone—especially Bryn. Devon sighed and looked at her stack of homework. Now if she could just come up with as much creative energy for her history essay.

don't think this is working," Cassidy told the DG on Friday. Just like the previous week, they were meeting at Costello's for coffee after school, although this time they were supposed to give their weekly progress reports. With only two weeks until homecoming, Cassidy was getting worried. So far this week had felt like a wash to her.

"How can you say that?" Bryn asked her. "I've made serious progress on my project." She grinned at Abby. "This afternoon, Kent told me that he's 'always admired you.'"

"Admired me?" Abby's dark eyes grew worried.

"Yeah. That's what he said. What? Are you complaining?"

"No . . . I mean, that's fine and good," Abby conceded. "But does he think I'm hot?"

Bryn laughed. "Do you want me to ask him *that*?"

"No, of course not." Abby firmly shook her head.

Bryn held up her phone. "I'm willing to call him and—"

"All right!" Devon pounded her fist on the table, causing

Cassidy's coffee to nearly topple. "Can this meeting come to order?"

"Bet you bring your gavel next time," Abby teased Devon.

"Yeah." Bryn frowned. "I thought we were supposed to have fun with this."

"We are. But you guys are getting sidetracked."

"I thought we were supposed to report," Bryn defended herself. "That's what I'm doing."

"Yeah." Devon held up her notebook. "But in an orderly fashion. And slow down so Cassidy can take notes." She handed the notebook to Cassidy.

"Why do we need to take notes?" Cassidy dug out a pen from her bag, then flipped through the pages.

"This is a club, isn't it?" Devon pointed out.

"I thought it was a game," Bryn said.

"Whatever." Devon shook her head. "Let's all report. One at a time. Then we'll make our next plan."

"Okay, since I began, is it all right if I continue?" Cassidy asked.

"Yes." Devon nodded eagerly. "Proceed."

Some of them giggled, but Cassidy *proceeded*. She admitted that she'd gotten nowhere with Harris. Then she made note of it, using their secret names.

"But you're supposed to be working on Harris for me," Devon reminded her with a disappointed expression. "You promised."

"I know that," Cassidy told her. "I'm trying. But I've barely been able to have a conversation with him, and even then he acted like I was invisible, and—"

"See." Bryn held up her forefinger with a smug look. "That's exactly why you should've left Hunk to me."

"*Harris,*" Devon checked her. "Code names are for texting, email, or when others might be listening. Remember?"

"Whatever." Bryn pointed at Cassidy now. "Maybe the problem with you is your appearance, Cass."

"What happened to that makeover you were supposed to give her?" Devon demanded.

"Scheduling difficulties," Bryn explained. "First Abby and I were busy. Then on the one night we could do it, Cassidy bailed on us. Although we did give her some tips. She was supposed to work on some things." She grimly shook her head. "Although that obviously hasn't happened."

Cassidy pressed her lips together, trying not to show how much this hurt. Sure, it was easy for Bryn—Miss Perfect—to pick on her looks. But did Cassidy have to take it?

"Cassidy is pretty enough," Emma argued. "She just hides it too well. Kinda like I used to."

"Precisely why she needs that makeover," Bryn stated.

"But she keeps balking," Abby told the others.

"Fine," Cassidy snapped. "Give me a makeover. You've been yammering about it all week. Can I help it if the timing was wrong?"

Bryn leaned forward, offering a pretty smile. "We'll do it this weekend, Cass. Abby and I already have some good ideas and—"

"Great." Cassidy blinked to keep tears from coming. "I can hardly wait." She tried to look like she was focused on the notebook, but she wished this meeting was over.

"It'll be fun, Cass," Emma said gently. "You'll see. If it makes you feel any better, I felt just the same way. Now I couldn't be happier for the way Devon and Bryn helped me. You'll be glad too."

Abby reached over and fingered Cassidy's long, dark brown hair. "Nothing wrong with this. I mean, nothing a good trim and the right shampoo and conditioner can't help. Believe me, with hair like mine, I understand the importance of good hair products. And then you need to learn how to blow dry it better—you know, to give it more body."

"But your clothes." Bryn shook her head. "Grunge went out when we were in preschool."

"Thanks." Cassidy tightened her grip on the pen. "What if I'm not into fashion?"

"We can see that," Bryn told her. "I'm not saying you have to go out and buy a bunch of new clothes. I'm just saying we can do something more. Something to make you look like you *care* about yourself." She laughed lightly. "Because if you don't care for yourself, who will care about you? Certainly not Lane."

"I don't want to hurt your feelings," Emma said carefully, "but she's right. I haven't been making any progress with Lane. He sees you as a nice girl. Not girlfriend material."

"He actually said that?" Cassidy challenged. What about that time their eyes met? Had she imagined his interest?

"Not in those words. But I could tell that's what he meant."

Cassidy sighed. Emma was probably right. "What about the speech Mr. Worthington gave the guys? Maybe Lane just wants to honor that. Maybe Harris does too."

"I got the inside scoop on that too," Bryn told them. Suddenly the girls were all ears. "Kent told me."

Abby frowned. "So you've got Kent confiding in you now? Don't forget he's mine, Bryn."

"Hey, we were just talking as friends. Can I help it if he opened up?"

"Never mind," Devon told them both. "Tell us what he said."

"Well, it sounds like Emma's theory is right. Mr. Worthington did give the guys a speech. It actually sounds kind of sweet. Worthington warns them that although a lot of girls make purity pledges, it's up to guys to respect this."

Cassidy felt a small surge of relief. "That's pretty cool."

"Yeah." Bryn nodded. "Except for one thing."

"What's that?" Abby asked.

"The problem is that Worthington challenges the guys. He actually throws down a *real* gauntlet after his talk."

"Huh?" Devon was confused. "He throws down a glove?"

"That's what Lane said." Bryn raised her hand to demonstrate. "He said Worthington smacks it down on the stage, and then he challenges them."

"With what?"

"He challenges them to see how long they can abstain from girls and dating."

"I knew it." Emma nodded triumphantly.

"And they fall for it?" Devon looked stunned. "I mean, these are guys, right? Hot-blooded teenage guys."

"It sounds like Worthington makes it seem like a sport, like only the toughest guys can win at this game. He's like, '*If you're a real man, you can do this.*'" Bryn laughed. "But according to Lane, it never lasts too long."

"Will it last through homecoming?" Devon asked.

"I'm not sure." Bryn's mouth twisted to one side. "But I think if we want dates for that dance, we're all going to have to turn up the heat. ASAP."

"Good information gathering," Devon told her.

"Maybe this is the writing on the wall," Cassidy said in defeat. "I mean, do we really want to go against Worthington?"

The group got quiet now, like they were actually considering her words. Oddly enough, she hoped they didn't agree with her. Despite her protests and hurt feelings, she was actually starting to long for a makeover. Who didn't want a fresh start sometimes?

"Don't look at it like that," Devon finally said. "After all, the school promotes homecoming and the dance. Surely they expect us to have dates, don't they?"

"I remember hearing how a lot of kids went stag to the homecoming dance last year," Emma told her. "Girls with girls. Guys with guys."

"You're kidding." Devon grimaced.

"That's true," Bryn conceded.

Abby giggled. "Bryn and I went together last year."

"I never knew why it was like that. But a lot of couples seemed to pair off at the dance," Bryn explained. "Maybe that's when the guys kissed Worthington's challenge good-bye."

Emma shrugged. "Worst case scenario, we could go in a group."

"Like in middle school?" Bryn shook her head. "No way."

"You got that right," Devon declared. "We are so *not* going to the dance as a group."

"Maybe we won't be going at all." Cassidy sighed.

"No. You're wrong. We are all going to get dates." Devon pointed at the notebook. "But we might need a better battle plan."

"I'm in." Bryn nodded firmly. "Even if this war is against General Worthington himself, I plan to fight it."

Cassidy tried to feign enthusiasm as she made notes while the girls plotted and planned, strategizing ways to drop subtle hints through texting and Facebook throughout the weekend. The plan was that the intensity of the battle would heat up as the school week started. By midweek the hints would grow increasingly less subtle. The goal was to nail dates before the following weekend.

"That's really cutting it close," Devon declared.

"I'll say." Bryn frowned. "I wanted to go dress shopping this weekend."

"So did I," Abby told her.

"No reason we can't shop for dresses," Devon said as she reached for the notebook.

"But what if we don't get asked?" Cassidy queried.

"We'll get asked," Devon assured her.

"We can always save our receipts," Emma said quietly. "Just in case."

"Well, that sounds overwhelmingly confident," Bryn teased.

"Just being realistic." Emma twisted her coffee cup in her hands. "Besides, some of us are on tighter budgets than others. No way am I wasting money on a dress, even an inexpensive one, that I'm not going to wear at least once."

"I'm with you on that," Cassidy told her.

"Are you two in the club or not?" Devon demanded.

Emma and Cassidy both nodded.

"Then let's hear a little more optimism."

"That's right." Bryn pointed at Cassidy now. "And I expect you to come to my house tomorrow afternoon for your makeover."

"When are we going dress shopping?" Abby asked.

After a couple minutes of going over their schedules, it was finally agreed that Cassidy's makeover would be switched to the morning, and the five girls would go dress shopping in the afternoon. But as Cassidy was going home, she still had her doubts. Yes, she would cooperate with the makeover. The more she thought about it, the more she felt her friends were probably right. But when it came to dress shopping, she would pace herself. It was fine if they wanted to make fools of themselves by purchasing formal dresses for a dance no one had invited them to. But she was not falling for it.

• • ● ● • •

"Do you think it's silly for me to get a makeover?" Cassidy asked her mom on Saturday morning.

Mom's brows lifted. "A makeover?"

"Nothing major," Cassidy said quickly. "I mean, I'm not cutting my hair or coloring it or anything drastic."

"Oh, good." Mom stroked Cassidy's hair. "Your hair is gorgeous."

"Yeah, my friends think it's my best asset."

Mom laughed. "Well, I think you have lots of assets."

Cassidy frowned. "So maybe I don't need a makeover?"

"You're getting a makeover?" Callie asked as she came into the kitchen.

Cassidy shrugged. This wasn't a topic she was eager to discuss in front of her pesky fourteen-year-old sister. After growing several inches and turning unexpectedly pretty (not that Cassidy planned to tell her, since her head was big enough), Callie had gotten obsessed with fashion.

"Well, if anyone could use a makeover, it would be you."

"Thanks a lot." Cassidy poured milk into her bowl of Cheerios.

"I'm not trying to offend you." Callie filled a bowl with granola cereal, measuring it carefully with her eyes, as if she thought one extra teaspoon might result in a pound. Callie's recent obsession with weight was ridiculous, bordering on scary. "Just being honest."

Cassidy turned back to Mom. "What do you think? I mean, in a spiritual way. Do you think God wants us to be all focused on our outward appearances?"

Mom smiled. "I think God prefers we work on our interior selves. But I also think there's nothing wrong with looking your best." She glanced at Callie. "As long as you don't take it to extremes."

"How do you know if you're taking it to extremes?" Cassidy asked. Mom wasn't just a mom. She was also a Christian counselor, and sometimes she was smarter than the average mom. Not always. But for the most part Cassidy respected her. A lot of times she even listened to her. Sure, her friends would probably think that was weird, but it was what it was.

"You have to stop and think," Mom said as she poured cream into her coffee. "Is your focus on appearances controlling you? Or are you controlling it? As soon as something—anything—starts pressing into your life and taking too much time and energy and ultimately controlling you . . . well, that's when it's time to stop and take stock."

Cassidy thought about this as she munched.

"Well, Cass doesn't need to worry about *that*," Callie said a bit glibly. "She has never been overly focused on her appearance."

"Unlike some people who will go unmentioned, Callie Marie." Cassidy gave her sister a slightly accusing look.

The comment must've gone right over her head, because Callie simply smiled as she tossed her shiny chestnut hair (which was similar to Cassidy's except that it was sleekly brushed and shimmered in the light). "Hey, I can't help it that I'm just naturally pretty."

"And not a bit conceited about it either," Cassidy said.

Mom gave Cassidy a warning look but said nothing.

"Just being honest," Cassidy mimicked her little sister as she rinsed her bowl in the sink.

"It's okay," Callie said lightly. "I'm used to girls being jealous."

Cassidy rolled her eyes as she set the bowl in the dishwasher.

"I hope you're more gracious to those girls than you are to your sister," Mom said. "A kind and gentle heart is much more attractive than a pretty face, Callie."

Callie gave Mom a look that said she'd heard that a million times before but didn't really believe it.

"She's fourteen," Cassidy said to Mom. "She'll grow out of this."

Callie made a sneering look now.

"Ooh, now that's really pretty," Cassidy said as she reached for her bag.

"Yes, and you're such an expert on pretty," Callie shot back.

"Girls!" Mom's voice had the edge of warning in it. She would tolerate only so much sibling bickering.

"I'll be gone most of the day," Cassidy told her.

"You did your chores?"

Cassidy nodded. "Callie still hasn't cleaned our bathroom. It's her turn today."

"Tattletale," Callie called out as Cassidy exited through the laundry room.

"Have fun," Mom called out, almost as if she wanted to cancel out Callie's bad manners.

"Thanks." As Cassidy went out to her car, she wondered if doing this makeover really was a good idea. What if she ended up as superficial and shallow as her little sister? Although that seemed ridiculous. It wasn't like her friends could turn back the clock and turn her into a snotty fourteen-year-old. Even so, as she drove over to Bryn's house, she promised herself that she would continue to focus on her inner self more than her outer self. No matter what her friends said or did.

Since Bryn had been only partially involved in Emma's fabulous makeover last weekend, she was even more determined to play an important role in Cassidy's. This was too much fun to miss out on. She'd known Cassidy for a few years now, and while she liked and respected her, she also knew that Cass could be pretty stubborn, not to mention negative sometimes. Cassidy liked to make fun of fashion and trends, acting like it was shallow for anyone to follow the fads. Maybe it was shallow, but Bryn liked it. She didn't need Cass to lecture her on why it was stupid.

As she flipped through her latest issue of *Teen Vogue* magazine, Bryn reminded herself that everyone was different—and that was okay. Besides, she actually respected that Cass took her Christian beliefs seriously, even if Bryn didn't. Oh, Bryn would go to church when her parents pressured her, but she didn't really embrace faith. Not like Cass did. She didn't quite get it either. What was the big deal? Even so, it was reassuring to know that Cass was like that—solid and dependable. Kind of like having an anchor. Except that an anchor dragged you down sometimes. Bryn tore out a couple pages of fashion dos and don'ts that she thought might be helpful for Cassidy. If she wouldn't listen to Bryn, maybe she'd listen to the experts.

It really bugged Bryn that Cass didn't seem to care about her appearance. Something was wrong with that. Even if Cassidy was just pretending not to care—although Bryn didn't know how that was possible—it was still pretty strange. What girl didn't want to look good? But sometimes Cassidy would come to school wearing the exact same outfit that she'd worn just a few days before. Was she that oblivious? Anyway, as far as Bryn was concerned, a makeover was long overdue. It would probably be therapeutic.

As Bryn did a quick straightening of her room, since this was to be the location of the makeover, she took a quick inventory of Cassidy in her head. It wasn't like Cass was unattractive. To be fair, she had a wholesome sort of attractiveness. Kind of like a farm girl. Despite Cassidy's blasé clothes, sloppy ponytails, and face always devoid of makeup, Bryn felt certain a pretty girl was lurking beneath. As she folded a pair of jeans—nicely fitting jeans, unlike the sloppy ones her frumpy friend usually wore—she imagined everything they would do to change Cassidy's image today.

Since Abby was about the same height as Cassidy, she was bringing over some clothes, so they could probably put together some fairly cool outfits. Abby and Bryn were the fashionistas of the group, and they had the closets to prove it. But Abby's hand-me-downs would only do so much. Cassidy would have to be willing to invest some too. Bryn had already told Cass to plan on spending a few bucks when they went shopping (beyond buying her dress for homecoming). Cass was reluctant to tap into her summer job earnings, but she had agreed. Devon had provided some hair product samples from her aunt, so that would save some money. And when it came to makeup, Bryn felt like she could handle it—at least she hoped so.

"Hey, sis." Tara stuck her head in Bryn's room. "What'cha got going today?"

Totally surprised to see her older sister, Bryn ran and hugged her. "Tara! What are you doing here?"

"I came home for the weekend."

Bryn looked into Tara's big blue eyes. They were almost the same color as Bryn's, and sometimes the two girls had even been confused as twins. "I'm so happy to see you. How's college?"

Tara let out a tired little groan. "It's mostly pretty cool. But I plan to catch up on some sleep this weekend. My roommate is the worst." She looked around the tidy room and at the bundle of clothes and hangers Bryn had dropped. "Cleaning house, are we?"

Bryn laughed. "Not really. Just picking up a little. I have some friends coming over." She proceeded to tell about to-day's makeover plans.

"You're redoing plain Jane Cassidy Banks?" Tara asked.

Bryn nodded. She was tempted to tell Tara about the DG but remembered their vow of secrecy. "We're all going to the homecoming dance, and we thought Cass could use a little help. After the makeover we're going dress shopping."

"Wow. Sounds like fun." She sighed. "And exhausting."

"I hope we don't disturb you."

"If it gets too loud, I'll go down to the family room to

sleep." Tara peered curiously at Bryn. "Who's taking you to homecoming? I didn't even know you had a boyfriend. And I just talked to Mom a couple days ago."

Bryn made a stiff smile. "He's not exactly a boyfriend . . . yet."

"Who?"

"Do you remember Jason Levine?"

Tara's eyes lit up. "Oh, yeah. That guy was a hottie. Even though he was a junior last year, he caught my eye. But I thought he had a girlfriend."

"He did. Amanda Norton. But they broke up. This year he's even hotter."

Tara gave Bryn a sly look. "Good going, girl. You're making your older sister proud."

Bryn tried to act natural, like this date with Jason was really a done deal. "It's all still pretty new," she said nervously. "No one really knows about it yet."

Tara laughed. "Well, don't worry about me. There's no one I talk to who hangs around Northwood anyway." She started to go, then paused. "Hey, if you need any help with your makeover, just yell."

"Seriously?" Bryn was surprised. "I thought you were tired."

"I am. But who can resist a good makeover? Remember the first time I started helping you?"

Bryn smiled. "Yeah. I still appreciate it."

"If you need my expertise, just let me know."

Bryn nodded and said she appreciated the offer, but she hoped she wouldn't have to call on her older sister for help. This was something she really wanted to accomplish on her own. Well, with a little help from Abby too. She looked at her watch. Abby should be here by now.

To Bryn's dismay, Cassidy arrived first. It didn't help matters that Cassidy seemed to be digging in her heels. "I'm not sure this is such a great idea," Cass said when they were in Bryn's room.

"But you agreed to—"

"I know. But I've never been the superficial type. All this focus on looks is kinda creeping me out. I was thinking on my way over here that if I have to change my appearance just to get Lane to look my way . . . well, it seems wrong. I mean, if he's going to like me, he's going to like me for who I am. Right?"

Bryn nodded hopelessly. "Right, but—"

"So I really don't see the point."

Just then Bryn's phone rang. It was Abby, informing her that she was going to be at least an hour late. "My mom's car is in the shop and—"

"Yeah, yeah. Never mind," Bryn said impatiently. "Just get here as soon as you can, okay?" She hung up feeling aggravated.

"Sounds like it's not going to work out." Cassidy was reaching for her bag.

"Don't leave yet," Bryn insisted. She remembered Tara's offer. "Let me get my sister and—"

"Tara's here?"

"Yeah. She just popped in. She actually offered to help with the makeover, but I didn't think I'd need her."

Cassidy's eyes lit up a little, and Bryn suddenly remembered that Tara had worked as a junior counselor at church camp one year and how Cassidy had really admired her. Maybe Tara would be just the ticket. "I'll be right back."

She hurried down to Tara's room, knocking lightly in case

she'd already gone to sleep. When she opened the door, it looked like Tara was just sorting her laundry. "What's up?" Tara asked.

Bryn quickly explained her dilemma. "Cassidy had been on board before," she said finally. "But now she's threatening to walk."

"Hmm . . ." Tara's brow creased.

"So if your offer was genuine . . . ?"

Tara sighed, then glanced down at her piles of clothes. "I really need to get this done before I go back." She smiled. "But if you're willing to work on my laundry, I'd be happy to work on Cassidy."

Bryn wasn't sure she liked this deal, but at the same time she didn't want Cassidy to slip away without her makeover. If the DG was going to work and if all the girls were going to get dates to homecoming, it seemed obvious that Cass would have to clean up her act. "Okay. I'll do it."

"Great." Tara went over to her dresser and picked up a bag. "Cassidy is in luck because I just got some new skin care stuff. I haven't even tried it yet. Maybe Cass and I can both have facials." She pointed to the mess of clothes. "You get started on this, and I'll get started on Cassidy."

As Bryn headed to the laundry room for baskets, she questioned her agreement. Was she a total fool to fall for this? Doing Tara's laundry—which looked like about three weeks' worth—was no small task. Still, if Cassidy came out looking good . . . maybe it would be worth it.

By the time Bryn got the clothes sorted and the first load in, then hurried back to her room, both Cassidy and Tara had green stuff on their faces. "Lovely," she teased as she flopped down on the bed.

"Can you go find us some cucumber slices?" Tara asked Bryn.

"That's okay, I'm not hungry," Cassidy said.

"For our eyes," Tara told her.

Bryn reluctantly agreed. Feeling a bit like Cinderella catering to the two green-faced stepsisters, she headed back downstairs and foraged through the fridge in search of a cucumber. After she found one, she cut four generous slices and took them back upstairs. Tara had taught her the cucumber trick years ago. It was supposed to reduce puffiness around the eyes. Not that Bryn had ever noticed any puffiness around her own eyes, but it always felt and smelled cool and fresh, and she almost wished she'd cut some pieces for herself.

"Here you go, ladies." She handed them the cuke slices, watching as they placed them over their closed eyes. As they relaxed with their strange-looking masks, she decided to check Facebook. She was working on Kent for Abby now, and she suspected that when Abby arrived, she would question Bryn on her progress. Bryn just hoped to have something positive to say.

To her relief, Kent had responded to her last message, and judging by his response, he was interested in Abby for more than just friendship. He thought she was hot! Well, he hadn't actually used the word *hot*, but Bryn could read between the lines. She shot back a quick playful response, trying to make it sound like he would be lucky to be with Abby. She also hinted that Abby wanted to go to the homecoming dance and if Kent just sat on his hands, he might miss out on this great opportunity. Then she crossed her fingers and hit Send.

With her portion of the work done, she would have no problem asking Abby how she was coming along with Jason now. Of course, she couldn't have this conversation in front of Tara since Tara assumed Bryn's date with him was a done deal—it would be humiliating. But she could get Abby alone for this info exchange. Bryn tried to appear confident amongst her friends, but she felt insecure when it came to Jason. Maybe she was a fool to go after him like this.

However, she wasn't blind. She had been noticing that she was getting more and more attention from other guys—including all the boys the other DG girls had set their sights on, which was admittedly fun. So why was it so difficult to get Jason to glance in her direction? Was it Worthington's speech? Or was he just not into her? Worse yet, what if Jason was still into Amanda?

Bryn knew from books and movies that when a guy was stuck on his ex, she was tough competition. What if Amanda decided to get back with Jason? Then it would be utterly hopeless. How humiliating would it be for the hottest girl in their club (as her friends kept suggesting) to be the lonely girl on the sidelines? How would it feel to be sitting at home the night of the dance? It was almost too much pressure.

That meant she needed to pressure Abby. As much as she hated to push her best friend, she realized it was time to nail this thing. She didn't want to be left out, so if it wasn't going to work with Jason, she would have to start working on a different guy. However, that would be tricky with Tara around. She would wonder why Bryn didn't go with Jason. And Bryn didn't like to lie. Not to her sister or anyone else. She hated to admit it, but maybe this Dating Games club was a big, stupid mistake.

Hearing someone downstairs, Bryn suspected that Abby had arrived and decided to run down and head her off before she said anything in front of Tara. Bryn's mom had just let Abby in, and they were exchanging greetings.

"Sorry to be late," Abby told Bryn. "Here are the clothes."

"It's okay." Bryn took the bags, setting them down on the bench by the door. "We don't need those yet." She pulled Abby toward the basement stairs, explaining how Tara was helping. "I need to talk to you first anyway." Leading Abby down to the family room where they could speak privately, Bryn said they needed to talk about Jason.

"Is something wrong?" Abby asked. "Have you decided to go with someone else?"

"No. I just need to know how it's going." Bryn sat down on the sectional. "I want an update. After my update, I'll tell you how it's going with Kent."

Abby's eyes lit up. "You've heard something new?"

"Sit down." Bryn patted the seat. "And talk. Tell me what you've done."

"Well, I contacted him on Facebook like you asked. He agreed to be friended. Then I sent him a message—just talking about sports in general, you know, so he won't be suspicious. This morning I saw that he responded. Just polite, but I can tell he's curious about why I friended him." Abby frowned. "I'm not sure where to go with it now."

"Just get to the point," Bryn urged. "But do it in such a way that he doesn't know you're doing it."

"That's easier said than done."

"Oh, I don't know . . ." Bryn gave her a mysterious smile.

"Why? What?"

"Kent is coming around, Abby. If he invites you to the dance, you will owe me big-time."

"Really?" Abby grinned. "You think he likes me?"

Bryn nodded. "I think you have a real chance with him."

"Cool."

"But I want you to get through to Jason too. I will be so humiliated if I'm the only one who doesn't go—"

"That's ridiculous. Of all the girls, you have the best chance of being asked, Bryn."

"By Jason?"

Abby looked concerned. "I . . . I don't know."

"See what I mean? What if I set my sights too high? What if he still likes Amanda? I've got to get this figured out. ASAP."

"Want me to work on it now?" She pulled out her iPhone.

Bryn shrugged. "I don't know. We don't want to look too anxious. But do it sometime today. Don't let him slip away, Abby."

Abby nodded grimly. "I promise I'll do all I can." Suddenly her serious expression melted into an excited smile. "Now tell me more about your conversations with Kent. *Please.*"

Bryn entertained Abby for a while by talking about Kent, then said, "Maybe you should go check on Cassidy. Take the clothes up there. In the meantime, I'll check on Tara's laundry."

"Tara's laundry?"

Bryn rolled her eyes. "My part of the agreement. I get to do a ton of laundry while Tara works on Cass."

"Why aren't you working on her?"

"Cass started freaking on me, acting like she wasn't going to cooperate. When I mentioned Tara was here and willing to help, Cassidy did an about-face. She trusts Tara. Anyway, as much as I don't enjoy doing laundry, it seemed like a good deal."

Abby patted her on the back. "You're truly a good friend,

Bryn. Washing your sister's dirty clothes in order to get a friend a makeover. There'll probably be a jewel in your crown in heaven for your self-sacrifice."

Bryn laughed. "Yeah, right." They parted ways at the laundry room, and Bryn started meticulously sorting through Tara's damp laundry, deciding what should go in the dryer and what should be hung up to dry. She and Tara had been doing their own laundry for ages now—ever since Mom went back to work at their dad's real estate agency. Bryn had learned the hard way, after shrinking some of her own favorite threads, not to just dump everything into the dryer. This was as critical as the presort and selecting the proper wash cycle.

Trying not to feel too left out—or like Cinderella—Bryn was determined to do a good job with Tara's laundry. What were sisters for if not to help each other? She just hoped that whatever Tara was doing to Cassidy would help the cause of the DG. More than that, she hoped that the DG would come through for her by snagging her a date with Jason. It would be so cool to walk into the dance with Jason by her side. As she sorted the clothes, she imagined herself with him. They would make a striking couple. She knew they would turn heads as they walked in together—that is, if they did walk in together. This deal was so not sealed yet. The DG had better not let her down!

By the time she finished in the laundry room and went back to her room, Tara was already working on Cassidy's makeup, and Abby was combing something into her hair. Progress was being made.

"Wow," Bryn said as she went around to look at Cass face-to-face. "You already look lots better."

"Really?" Cassidy looked dubious. "I'll admit that my skin felt better after the mask came off. That is, until Tara started putting that goop on."

"That *goop* is an amazing combination of moisturizer and foundation that looks natural and creamy." Tara stepped back to admire her work. "It evens out your skin tone and covers imperfections."

"Like zits?" Cassidy said hopefully.

"We call them blemishes," Tara primly corrected her. "Fortunately, you don't have many."

"Hey, that's really working." Bryn nodded with approval. "That spot on her chin is almost invisible now."

"Can I see?" Cassidy asked.

"Not yet." Tara shook her head.

"Well, how will I know how to do this myself if I don't watch what you're doing to me?" Cassidy complained.

"Abby has been taking notes, and I'll make a list of what you need to get," Tara told her as she started working on Cassidy's eyes.

Abby pointed to a tablet on the dresser. "It's all right there."

"I don't want to look overly made-up," Cassidy warned. "I want to look natural."

"I know. I know." Tara sounded aggravated. "You've only said that like a million times."

"Your hair needs a trim," Bryn told Cassidy. "Your ends are really split and broken. If you want I can do it. Or maybe Tara can. We've both trimmed each other's hair enough times to know what we're doing. Right, Tara?"

"Yeah, but you're better with the scissors than I am," Tara said as she took tweezers to Cassidy's eyebrows. "In fact, maybe you can give me a trim too, before I go back to school."

"Ouch!" Cass let out a screech and jumped up. "What are you doing?"

"Thinning this unibrow."

"I do *not* have a unibrow." Cassidy rubbed her forehead.

"Okay, that's an exaggeration, but you do have really bushy brows, girlfriend. And they are frighteningly close to each other in the middle. Trust me, Cass, they need a serious plucking. Get back in the chair."

"I don't want to look like a freak." Cassidy hesitantly sat back down. "I mean, I've seen girls who plucked so much of their brows that they looked like aliens."

"Don't worry," Bryn assured her. "Tara is an expert at brows. She even does my mom's for her."

Cassidy let out a loud groan each time Tara pulled a single hair. "Why does it have to be so painful?"

"The price of beauty," Tara said without sympathy.

Once Abby had Cassidy's hair combed and smoothed, Bryn went for the scissors and plugged in the curling iron. Judging by those frazzled ends, it would be more than just a tiny trim like she'd promised, but Bryn was determined not to take off more than two or three inches. Just enough to put some bounce back into it. As she clipped, she and Abby both gave Cass a mini-lecture about proper conditioning habits for long hair.

"I just don't see the point," Cassidy argued. "I mostly keep it in a ponytail anyway."

Tara rolled her eyes at Bryn. "That is *exactly* the point."

"Huh?" Cassidy looked confused, and Bryn couldn't help but laugh. How could a girl be so totally clueless?

"Maybe the ponytail is getting a little old," Abby said. "I mean, it's cool for sports and around the house and stuff, but every day?"

"Seriously," Bryn said to Cass as she trimmed. "If a girl wants to have long hair, she should accept that there's some maintenance involved."

"That's right," Abby agreed. "You should see how much time it takes to get my hair smoothed out like this. It's an investment."

"An investment?" Cassidy frowned. "I thought it was just hair. What's the big deal anyway?"

"Maybe you should just shave it off then." Tara held the tweezers in front of Cassidy's nose. "Or I could pluck it all out for you."

They all laughed.

"Don't you guys think it's pretty weird how you focus so much on appearances?" Cass asked the others. "Haven't you heard that beauty is only skin deep? What about your minds? What about your talents? How about focusing on those things for a change?"

"We *do* focus on those things," Abby said defensively. "You know that, Cassidy. Don't get on your soapbox with us. You know good and well that we all have interests besides our looks. But some people completely neglect their appearances, and then it's time for an intervention."

"Not that we're naming names, *Cassidy Banks*." Bryn chuckled as she combed out the ends of Cassidy's hair to see if they were even.

It was early afternoon when they finished Cass's makeover. Tara had worked magic on her face before she slipped off to catch a nap. Abby and Bryn had finished with her hair and then helped to outfit her in some of Abby's clothes.

"Time for the big reveal," Bryn said proudly as she led Cassidy to the full-length mirror on the inside of her closet door. Made over from head to toe, Cass looked like a new person. Her brown hair looked shiny and healthy and full of body. Her skin looked fresh and natural—but pretty. And her outfit really took her overall image up quite a few notches.

"Voilà!" Bryn said as she opened the door for Cass to see.

"No way . . ." Cassidy leaned forward to peer at herself. "Is that really me?"

"A new and improved you," Abby told her.

"Wow." Cassidy seemed surprisingly impressed.

"Wow is right." Bryn tugged her down the hallway. "I told Tara we'd show her how you turned out. I'll knock quietly in case she's sleeping."

After they shared their success with Tara, Bryn called Devon to see where they were supposed to meet to look for dresses. "We'll be there around 2:00," she told her. "Wait until you see Cassidy's new look."

"Great," Devon said. "We've already scouted some really great-looking gowns. Oh yeah, and Emma has some good news for Cassidy." Her voice was laced with promise.

"About Lane?"

"Yep."

"Already?" Bryn felt slightly dismayed. "But he hasn't even seen her since the makeover."

"I guess he liked her just the way she was."

Bryn groaned and lowered her voice. "Well, let's not mention that to her, okay?"

"Sure . . . whatever. See you in a bit."

Bryn tucked her phone into her bag and shook her head. Hopefully all their work on Cassidy wasn't for nothing. Surely a guy wouldn't be less interested in a girl just because she'd improved her appearance . . . would he?

Abby tried to keep up with her best friend, Bryn, in the fashion arena, but sometimes it could be challenging to say the least. Keeping up with Bryn in the shopping arena could prove downright exhausting, and Abby was an athlete too! By the time Bryn called it quits, the DG had put in nearly five hours at the mall. When Abby got home, she was as worn out as if she'd competed in a cross-country race. Her one consolation, however, was that with Bryn's help, she had managed to snag a very cool dress.

"I saved some dinner for you," Mom called as Abby came into the house. "Your dad got takeout from Thai-Spoon. Your favorite."

"Thanks, I'm starved." Abby held up the pale pink garment bag like it was a trophy. "I found my dress."

Mom looked up from where she was working on her laptop in the dining room and made a surprised frown. "You mean for homecoming? You already *got* a dress?"

Abby was unzipping the bag now. "Yeah. Everyone said it looked so great on me, and it fit absolutely perfectly. I was afraid if I didn't get it, someone else might snatch it up."

Mom stood and came over with a worried look. "Well, let's see."

Abby extracted the long, dark purple dress from the bag.

"Eggplant . . ." Mom nodded with an uncertain expression.

"Huh?"

"The color. It's eggplant."

"Oh, well . . . yeah, I guess so." Abby held up the dress in front of her like she was wearing it.

"Where are the straps?" Mom sounded alarmed. "Abby, you know good and well that the school has a code for dances. No strapless dresses allowed—period."

"Don't worry." Abby fished down inside the dress and pulled up a strap that went across the front and over one shoulder to the back. "See?"

"*One* strap?" Mom frowned.

"It's a pretty wide strap," Abby said, defending herself. "Honestly, I think this strap has three times as much fabric as the straps on the dress that Bryn got today. It's very secure."

"Abby . . . I don't know . . ."

"It's okay," Abby assured her. "Bryn told me that her sister Tara wore one almost exactly like this to prom last year. No problem whatsoever."

"No problem . . . Well, wait until your dad sees it, then we'll see if it's a problem or not. In the meantime, hold on to your receipt."

"Don't worry." Abby already had the receipt safely tucked into her wallet. Not because of parental approval, but just in case she didn't get asked to the dance after all.

Mom shook her head. "You're lucky your father's at a meeting tonight."

Despite the threat in Mom's voice, Abby didn't feel too worried as she slid the dress back into the bag. Knowing Dad and how busy he'd been lately, he probably wouldn't see this dress until the night of the dance, and by then it would be too late. She hung the dress over the top of a door, then went to the fridge to dig out the little white cartons. But when she turned around, Mom was still standing there, looking a bit forlorn.

"I was really looking forward to going dress shopping with you," Mom told her as Abby dumped what was left of the pad Thai onto a plate.

Abby slid the plate into the microwave and turned around. "I'm sorry, Mom. It's just that you're always so buried with work and stuff . . . I just figured you'd appreciate that I took care of this on my own." Abby's parents had always valued independence.

"Well, yes, of course, I'm glad you took care of it yourself. But as a mom—and don't forget, you're my only daughter . . ." She shrugged. "Well, I'd imagined us doing that together. A mother-daughter thing."

Abby looked into her mom's eyes. "Oh, Mom, I'm really sorry," she said sincerely. "I didn't realize it was that big of a deal for you."

Mom looked sad.

Abby went over and hugged her. "Seriously, Mom, if I'd known it meant that much to you, I would've waited. But after spending the whole afternoon shopping with four other girls, I was so relieved to find the right dress that I just had to get it." She smiled. "And it was a really good deal too."

Mom brightened a little. "Really?"

"Yeah." The bell on the microwave dinged, and Abby pulled out the hot food. "I actually found it at one of the discount stores. We were trying to shop some inexpensive places for Emma—she's on a pretty tight budget. I couldn't believe it when I saw it. I'd tried on a dress almost exactly like it at Nordstrom's, and it was almost four times as much."

"Wow." Mom looked impressed. "Nice shopping."

Abby forked into the noodles and took a big bite.

"Did all the girls find dresses?"

"Uh-huh." She nodded. "It was pretty cool, actually. Bryn sort of managed the whole thing, and by the time we finished up, everyone was happy."

"That's quite an accomplishment. Five girls shopping at once and everyone finds a dress. I'm impressed."

Abby took another bite, hoping that Mom wouldn't inquire about their dates for the dance. Ironically, it seemed easier to find a dress for the dance than a guy to go with. Not that she planned to mention this. "I still need to get shoes," she said suddenly. "Maybe you and I could shop for those together."

"Shoe shopping." Mom grinned. "That would be such fun. Don't you dare go without me."

"All right." Abby picked up her plate. "Do you mind if I take this to my room? I have some homework to catch up on."

Mom tipped her head to her laptop. "Sure. I have some work to do too."

Relieved that Mom wasn't asking more about plans for the dance, Abby took her plate in one hand and the dress in the other and headed to her room. It was true that she did have homework, but at the moment she was more focused on working on Jason for Bryn. He was her assignment, and after hearing about how much progress the other girls had been making, she felt guilty. It would be horrible if Bryn was the only one without a date for the dance. Not that it was likely. Most guys would be thrilled to take out a girl as hot as Bryn. What was wrong with Jason? As Abby turned on her computer, she wondered if she should start looking around for an alternate guy. It shouldn't be hard to find a willing date for someone like Bryn. Except that Bryn had her heart set on Jason.

To Abby's surprise, she had a message from Kent on Facebook. She set her dinner aside and clicked on it.

> Bryn says you girls want to go to homecoming. Gotta like a girl who speaks her mind and doesn't beat around the bush. What do you think? Is Bryn serious? Or is she just pranking me?

Abby read the message twice. It had been sent at 4:05 this afternoon. It was now 7:34. Too soon to respond? She didn't think so. Still, she wanted to do it carefully. Don't act too eager. Make him do the asking. These were things all five girls had agreed on when they had a late lunch in the food court today.

> Homecoming sounds like fun. And I can speak for all my female friends . . . we are definitely interested. But we hear that you guys might be under Worthington's thumb. Any truth to that rumor?

She hit Send, then returned to eating. She didn't expect him to get back to her any time soon. Nonetheless, later, as she was doing homework and sending a couple messages to Jason, she took time to check. She checked again and again and again. Finally, it was past 10:00 and she was just shutting down her computer when she noticed Kent had responded again.

You're asking me to give you top secret information. Let's just say that my buddies and me are capable of making up our own minds about certain things. If you like I'll run this idea past some of them and get back to you later this week.

She wrote back saying that sounded good but warning him not to wait too long, hinting like he might miss his big chance. Devon had told them to give the impression that it was possible the guys could be too late—that the girls might have other opportunities. As she hit Send, she hoped she hadn't gone too far. But Devon had made it clear—the way to hook a guy was by playing hard to get.

"Despite what they might say, guys like to feel like they're the hunters," Devon had explained as if she'd put a lot of research into this. "Not like they're being pursued."

"That's right," Bryn had agreed. "We need to make them feel like we're not that interested. And like we have other options."

"Why do we have to play games?" Cassidy demanded.

"This is the Dating Games," Devon reminded her.

"But it feels so weird," Cassidy complained. "Why can't we just be open and honest?"

"Because it will backfire on you," Devon declared.

"What makes you such an expert?" Cassidy demanded. "How many dates have you actually been on anyway?"

"Are you questioning me?" Devon looked offended.

"Look," Bryn said gently. "Devon's right. That's exactly what I've seen my sister do—play hard to get—and she's got a pretty good track record for luring guys in. Don't you think?"

"It's true," Abby assured them. "I've seen it myself. Tara has a real gift for getting guys to go after her."

"I suppose it has nothing to do with her looks . . ." Cassidy shook her head like she was still unconvinced.

"Besides Tara, it's what you see on movies and TV," Emma said, a bit uncertainly. "The girl that's hard to get usually gets the guy. It makes sense to me."

"Like movies and TV are for real." Cassidy frowned.

"What about *The Bachelor*?" Devon said. "It's a *reality* show. And the girls frantically chasing after the guy are usually the ones who don't get a rose and get sent home."

"You honestly take that show seriously?" Cassidy rolled her eyes.

"All I'm saying is that none of us wants to come across as desperate and clingy and pathetic," Bryn said firmly. "I know I don't. Are you saying you do, Cass?"

Cassidy backed down at that point, admitting that she didn't want to look desperate either.

"So despite that we don't have dates and we're out shopping for dresses . . ." Bryn chuckled over this. "We will promise to each other not to act desperate."

Right then they'd all lifted their right hands and pledged to this. As far as Abby could see, she was holding up her end of the bargain now. Even so, she had an underlying feeling of desperation as she made room for the formal gown in her closet. It was so pretty, and it would be so fun to wear it. Just the same, she was not throwing away the receipt, although the clerk had said there was only a seven-day grace period, and only if the dress had never been worn. As gorgeous as the dress was, she knew she'd never wear it without a date. She just hoped she'd get the chance to wear it. If only Kent would cooperate.

Devon called her dad on Sunday morning. It had been a couple months since she'd last spoken to him, but she had a reason for calling today. Plain and simple—she wanted money.

"Mom says you're late on child support," Devon told him. *"Again."* She could tell she woke him up. Not that she cared much since it was already past 10:00.

"Hello to you too," he said groggily. "So nice to hear your voice."

"Sorry, Dad." She softened her tone. "It's just that it's not easy being in this private school. I have a whole new set of friends, and I have to be able to measure up. There's this big dance coming up. Homecoming. I want to go, and I used all my money to buy the dress, which is really great, but now I'm broke, and I don't even have shoes yet. Plus there are some other expenses too. I need help."

He let out a low groan.

"I'm really sorry to bug you." She spoke even more sweetly. "But if you could just send me some cash, I'll beg Mom not to put too much pressure on you for being late with the child support." Okay, she realized she was stepping way over the line here. But she also knew that Mom had a very good job. Better than Dad's. And sometimes Devon wondered about the fairness of Dad getting stuck with so much of the financial responsibility. She and Mom had gotten the house and the best car, while Dad was living in a tiny apartment downtown. However, she reminded herself, he was the one who chose to leave, and although it had never been said, Devon was pretty sure that it was because of a woman.

"So . . . how much do you need?" he asked slowly.

She gave him a generous number, certain that he'd balk at it. But when he didn't, she gratefully thanked him and promised to work on Mom. "I'll email you some photos of me in my homecoming dress," she said finally.

"I wish I could be there to see you," he said sadly.

"Me too." Then she told him to have a good day and hung up. Having parents split like this was painful. At least she was learning how to use it to her advantage . . . sometimes. Most of the time, she would gladly give up everything and anything just to have her parents happily married again. However, she knew the likelihood of that was probably comparable to winning the lottery. So not happening.

Her parents had acted like because she was a teenager, and in their opinion nearly grown, she shouldn't really care that they were divorcing. Like she had her own life and would soon be off in college—la-di-da. Like it didn't matter that she no longer had a house with two parents to come home to. And what about Christmas and other holidays? Or special times like the homecoming dance or graduation? Or what if she got married someday? How would they handle her wedding? Naturally, they didn't think about those things. Or maybe they just didn't want to talk about them.

Devon checked her phone, hoping she might have a text from Cassidy, since Cass was the one supposedly working on Harris for her, but she had nothing from Cassidy. Although it had been Devon's choice to switch Harris from Bryn to Cassidy—for obvious reasons—she now questioned the wisdom of this. At least Bryn had been trying, although Devon had been uncertain as to who Bryn was working for—herself or Devon. Meanwhile, it didn't look like Cassidy was even lifting a finger to help. Why should she be surprised? Cass was the biggest heel-dragger of the group. Devon wondered why they'd even let her join.

Devon decided to text Cassidy. A gentle nudge couldn't hurt. Even if Cass was in church right now, which was prob-ably the case, Devon knew that some of her friends received and sent text messages while in church. Maybe if Cassidy was bored enough, she'd take the time to send something to Harris. Devon could only hope.

• • ● • •

On Monday what little patience Devon had for Cassidy was quickly evaporating. Despite Cass getting her great makeover and the fact that Emma had made serious progress in getting Lane's attention for her, Cass was definitely slacking. It was just wrong that Cassidy should benefit from the DG without even lifting a finger.

By noon, Devon had decided to give her a piece of her mind. She started by reading rules two and three to her during lunch. "Two: *We will be loyal to our fellow DG members.* And three: *We will help fellow DG members to find dates with good guys.*" She narrowed her eyes at Cassidy. "Can you honestly say you're doing that?"

Cassidy's neatly plucked brows arched. "What are you saying?"

"I'm saying you're not making any progress with Harris for me. Yet we've all been working to help you. In case you haven't noticed, you seem closer to nailing a date to the dance than anyone else in the DG. It's just not fair."

Cassidy frowned. "I'm sorry. What do you want me to do?"

"Invest yourself," Devon told her. "Act like you care."

Cassidy shrugged. "Okay."

"Listen," Bryn said quietly. "We do need to work together, but we also need to keep things light. Remember, *we are not desperate.*"

Devon took in a deep breath. She knew Bryn was right. Even so, she felt slightly desperate. "But Harris still doesn't even know I'm alive." She glanced over to where Harris and Isaac were just coming out of the lunch line. "When I said hi to him today, he didn't even respond."

"Why don't you let me work on Harris for you," Bryn offered. "It seemed like I was getting somewhere with him last week."

Devon wasn't so sure.

"How about if I work on him?" Emma offered. "After all, it looks like I've succeeded with Lane." She glanced at Cassidy. "Right?"

Everyone stared at Cassidy, and her expression was a mixture of embarrassed and smug. "Yeah . . . I guess so. Lane has really started talking to me. But so far no invite to the dance yet."

Emma turned to Devon. "I sort of have a connection with Harris—I mean, since he's best friends with Isaac. Did I tell you that I seem to be making real progress with Isaac? He actually talked to me this morning—and I didn't initiate it either." Emma beamed at them. "It felt like he was really interested in me."

Cassidy looked surprised. "You didn't tell me that."

"I was going to, but it just happened and—"

"Back to Harris." Devon pointed at Emma. "Yes, I'd like your help."

"What about me?" Bryn asked. "Abby is supposed to be working on Jason for me, but so far—no offense, Abby—but we're not making progress."

"I just need a little more time," Abby assured her. "Give me a day or two."

"Maybe I can help," Devon told her. "Since it's going pretty well with Isaac now, I could focus my energy on Jason for you."

"Would you?" Bryn looked hopefully at her.

Devon smiled. Suddenly she saw the brilliance of this plan. If Bryn was dependent on Devon to secure a date with Jason, she wouldn't try to mess anything up with Harris. Would she?

They kicked around this new plan a bit more, making sure that they were all on the same page. Finally, satisfied that every girl was committed to the cause, Devon made another suggestion. "How about if we give this plan our full effort until Wednesday—that's a week and half before the dance. If no one has been asked by then, we'll regroup and revise our battle plan as needed." They all agreed to this, and as Devon went to her next class, she felt confident. Somehow they would pull this thing off. They had to!

• • ● • • •

It wasn't until Wednesday afternoon that Devon felt like she was making real progress with Jason. To her surprise, he waited to walk with her as she emerged from biology. He made it seem casual, but it felt set up to her. As they made small talk on their way to the locker bays, she experienced an odd sensation. Was she imagining things, or was Jason actually flirting with her? And if he was, did she really mind? He was awfully good looking. What would the harm be if he was interested in her? Maybe Bryn could go to the dance with Harris. Of course, she knew that rule six clearly outlawed stealing boyfriends. But was Jason really Bryn's boyfriend? They'd never gone out.

"So . . ." Jason eyed her with what seemed like approval. "You haven't even been here a month, and you're already stirring up trouble."

"*Moi?*" She giggled.

He looked amused. "Kent told me you're the one who got the girls all worked up about going to the homecoming dance."

She acted shocked. "Why would I do that?"

"To shake things up." He grinned.

She gave him a sly sort of smile. "What's wrong with shaking things up?"

He looked directly into her eyes with a surprising intensity. "Nothing much, I guess. Some things are better when shaken."

"So are you interested?" she asked. "I don't mean in me," she said quickly. "I mean just interested in general—not interested in me."

He laughed. "You sure about that? Sounds to me like you're asking me to take *you* to the dance."

"No. No." She firmly shook her head. Her cheeks suddenly got warm, and she almost felt like he'd been reading her thoughts. "I'm not asking for *me*. I mean, I'm not asking for *anyone*." She felt flustered, bumbling around like a seventh grader. She took in a quick steadying breath, faking a self-assured smile. "I'm just curious as to your interest level in general. That's all."

His smile grew larger. This guy seemed to ooze confidence, which was both attractive and aggravating. "Well, my interest level is steadily rising, Devon."

"You're not one of the guys who's worried about the Worthington speech?"

His brows arched. "You know about *that*?"

She glanced around uneasily. Had she just spilled state secrets? "Yeah . . . just a little."

"Well, I've never taken the Worthington speech too seriously." He chuckled. "I obviously wasn't influenced by it last year. I'm for sure not going there now. Not in my senior year." He leaned in closer. "And for sure not with girls like you around." His eyes seemed to run from her head to her toes and back up again—but all in the flash of a microsecond. Or maybe she'd just imagined it.

She felt a nervous flutter as she swallowed hard. This was not how this was supposed to go down. "I, uh, I heard you used to go with Amanda Norton," she said carefully. "Is that relationship really over?"

Jason's smile faded slightly as he made a noncommittal shrug.

"Because if it is," she continued, "I know of a certain girl who might be interested."

His smile returned. "A girl who's kind of new to this school?"

She waved her hand. "I'm serious, Jason. I'm not talking about myself."

He looked slightly confused. "Who then?"

"Bryn Jacobs," she said.

His look grew even more puzzled. "Bryn?"

She nodded.

He seemed honestly blindsided. "Not you?"

She shook her head.

"So you already have a date to the dance?"

"Well, no . . . not actually."

"Huh?"

"What do you think—are you interested in Bryn or not?"

He got a hard-to-read look, almost like a mix of disappointment and curiosity. "I'm gonna have to think about that one, Devon." He turned abruptly, heading toward the senior locker bay. Somehow this hadn't gone down quite like she'd anticipated. Yet at the same time she felt strangely flattered by his attentiveness.

Was it possible that a guy as cool as Jason was actually interested in her? From what she'd heard, Jason was considered the school's hottie. She'd assumed it would take a girl like Bryn Jacobs to snare him. But perhaps she had been wrong. Perhaps she'd set her sights too low in settling for Harris.

Of course, this posed a serious problem. For one thing, there were the DG rules. Here they were barely out of the gates, and she was considering breaking them—the rules of a club she'd worked so hard to establish. No, Devon decided as she opened her locker, she needed to come at this from a different angle.

"Hey, Devon."

She turned to see Bryn peering curiously at her. "What's up?"

"Huh?" Devon slammed her locker shut, stuffing some books into her bag and trying to appear obliviously innocent.

"I mean with JT." Bryn smiled prettily.

"JT?"

"You know . . . code." She lowered her voice. "For Jason."

"Oh. Right."

"I noticed you talking to him."

"Oh, yeah, I guess I was." Devon nodded like she was just remembering something insignificant, like maybe she'd just experienced a quick case of temporary amnesia.

"So?" Bryn's eyes twinkled. "Were you talking about *me*?"

"Yeah, as a matter of fact we were." Devon pulled the strap of her bag more snugly over her shoulder.

"And . . . ?" Bryn waited expectantly.

"And what?"

"What did he say?" Bryn's tone grew perturbed.

Devon glanced around the busy locker bay like she was uncomfortable. "You really want to have this conversation here?"

"Right." Bryn nodded like she got this. "Maybe not."

Devon promised Bryn they would talk later. In the meantime, she needed to come up with a new plan—to convince Bryn she should go after Harris instead of Jason. At least for this go-around. After all, hadn't Devon made it clear to all the members? The Dating Games were meant to be games—an arena where they could learn about dating. Did it really matter which guys they ultimately went out with? Besides that, everyone knew that rules were made to be broken.

Emma didn't know what to expect when she showed up at Costello's for the DG meeting. As far as she could tell, their club was turning into a disaster. Bryn was upset that Jason seemed to have gotten interested in Devon. Abby thought that Kent was interested in Bryn. Emma was still waiting for Isaac to step up to the plate. Ironically, it seemed that Cassidy was the only one enjoying a little success. Emma had witnessed the whole thing, and although she was glad for Cassidy's sake, she was feeling left out.

"Can you believe it?" Cass chirped happily as they sat down at Costello's with the other girls. "Lane asked me to the dance."

"When did this happen?" Abby asked.

"Just a few minutes ago in the school parking lot." Cassidy beamed at them. "I guess the DG really works."

"Maybe for you," Emma said glumly.

"This is so not fair," Bryn complained to Cass. "You do

129

the least work of any of us, and then you're the one who lands the first date. *How is that fair?*"

Cassidy just shrugged.

"Well, it's not over yet," Devon told them. "It's possible that we just need to regroup. That's why I called this meeting."

"Regroup as in you stealing Jason from me," Bryn said hotly. She set her cup down so firmly that her mocha sloshed over the side.

"I am not stealing anyone," Devon told her. "Can I help it if he's more into me than you?"

"What about the rules?" Bryn demanded.

"That's right." Cassidy pointed at Devon's notebook, which was sticking out of her bag. "Already you guys are breaking them."

"That depends on how you interpret them," Devon argued as she removed the notebook. "For instance, answer this for me: Is Jason Bryn's *boyfriend*?" She looked around the table, and everyone appeared uncertain. Emma had to agree with Devon on this. "See what I mean?" Devon pressed. "Bryn has never gone out with Jason, so how does that make him her boyfriend?"

"But we all know she was going *for* Jason," Abby told her.

"Yes, and we all know I was going for Harris. It looks like Harris is not interested in me." She pointed at Bryn. "But we know Harris is interested in you."

"And Jason is interested in you?" Cassidy asked Devon in disbelief.

Devon grinned. "Yeah, I think so."

Bryn folded her arms across her front, narrowing her eyes.

"We just need to keep things in perspective," Devon told them. "These are the Dating Games, which means this is like a sport. Does it really matter who takes you to the dance as long as you go?"

Emma wasn't so sure. "But what if I don't want to go with someone besides Isaac?"

"Why not?" Devon demanded. "Maybe Isaac would be more interested in you if he saw you with another guy."

Emma could barely imagine herself with Isaac. How would she possibly be comfortable with someone else?

"Back to Harris and Jason," Bryn said sharply.

Devon held up her hands helplessly. "What do you want me to do?"

"You used to like Harris," Abby quietly told Bryn. "Maybe it wouldn't be so bad going with him."

"But it feels like Devon stole Jason from me," Bryn argued. "Like I never even had a chance."

"For your information, I tried to talk Jason into taking you out," Devon told her.

"Right. Now you're acting like you had to force him to even consider it." Bryn stood up and grabbed her bag. "I think I've had enough of this club." She stormed off.

"I'd better go with her," Abby told them.

"See if you can talk some sense into her," Devon called as Abby hurried away.

Cassidy looked concerned. "What will I do if I'm the only one going to the dance?" she said suddenly. "I told my parents it was a group date. They won't like it if it's just Lane and me. Besides that, what if, thanks to Worthington's speech, no other guys want to go to the dance?"

"Don't worry so much," Devon said casually. "I'm pretty sure I'll be going to the dance. And I'm working on Isaac for you." She pointed at Emma. "I think he'll come around."

"Cassidy made a good point, though," Emma told her. "What if hardly anyone goes to the dance? Won't we look ridiculous? Maybe this is all a big mistake."

"Emma," Devon said sharply. "Don't be such a wet blanket." She scowled at Cassidy as she pulled out her iPhone. "I'm going to text Isaac the good news right now—that Lane and Cass are going. I'll insinuate that others are going too." She was texting something, but Emma couldn't see it. "I'll make it seem like he's going to be left out."

Cassidy's smile returned. "Good. Then even if it's just Emma and Isaac, at least it'll be a double date. My parents might be okay with that."

"This is not just about you," Devon told her.

Cassidy looked slightly guilty now. "Yeah, I know, but I don't see how I can help the others."

"You can," Devon said. "It's now up to you to put some pressure on Lane. Get out your phone and encourage him to get the other guys on board. Convince him that it'll be more fun if there are a bunch of us going together."

Emma nodded eagerly. "Yeah. Maybe he can talk to Isaac."

"That's right," Devon told Cass. "It's the least you can do for Emma. After all, if she hadn't talked to Lane, you probably wouldn't even have a date."

• • • • •

On Thursday morning, as Emma was on her way to art class, Isaac fell into stride right next to her. "What's the big hurry?" he asked in a friendly tone. "Where's the fire?"

Caught off guard, she gave him a shy smile. "No big hurry," she said, trying to remain calm. "What's up?"

"Not much." He pressed his lips tightly together, as if he

was about to say something but felt unsure. Feeling hopeful, she slowed down her pace and made a feeble attempt at small talk. They were nearly at the art room. If he didn't say something soon, this moment would be lost.

"So . . ." he said slowly. "I hear Lane is taking Cassidy to the dance."

Emma just nodded. "Yeah. I heard that too."

"And, well, I was wondering . . . maybe you'd like to go with me?"

Despite her wildly pounding heart, Emma was determined to remain calm. "Sure," she said quietly. "That'd be fun."

Isaac looked surprised. "So you do? You want to go?"

She laughed. "Didn't I just say so?"

He gave her an embarrassed smile. "Yeah, I guess you did. Okay, it's a date then."

"Yeah." With one hand on the art room door, she looked up into his sincere-looking blue eyes and gave him a happy smile. "It is."

"Cool." Just like that, he turned and hurried off. Emma felt so jazzed that she wanted to jump up and down and squeal like a four-year-old, but she managed to control herself until Isaac was out of sight. Once she saw him disappear around the corner, she did a little happy dance right there in the hallway before entering the art room. She didn't even care when some of the other art students teased her. It was worth it. She was going to the homecoming dance!

Emma couldn't wait to tell her friends, but since this was a no-phone time, she would have to contain her excitement until lunch. She'd be sure to show her gratitude to her DG friends, and she'd apologize for being so impatient with them, because it seemed obvious that it was working. As Emma began working on her charcoal sketch, she still could hardly believe that Isaac had asked her to the dance. If anyone had told her, back before the DG, that she would be going to the homecoming dance with Isaac McKinley, she would've chalked them up as just plain crazy. And yet . . . she was going. And she already had the dress!

On Thursday afternoon, as she emerged from the choir room, Cassidy was surprised to see that Lane was waiting for her. At least she assumed that was what he was doing since he smiled and waved.

"Going home now?" he asked.

"Yeah," she told him. "My car's in the other parking lot."

"Yeah, mine too. Mind if I walk with you?"

She laughed. "Of course not."

"I just finished with soccer practice and thought you might be having choir practice."

"Yeah, we've been practicing a lot lately. We have our jazz concert the week after homecoming."

"Speaking of homecoming . . . I kinda wanted to talk to you about that," he said quietly.

"Oh?" She glanced at him, noticing that he seemed rather glum. "Something wrong?"

"Sort of."

Disappointment washed over her. Was he getting ready to break their date? Tell her he changed his mind, that it was a mistake, or maybe even that it was a bad joke? How mean would that be? Even as these thoughts tumbled through her head, she thought she probably deserved this. First of all, she was the one who'd been so negative about the DG. Then when she was the first one to land a date, she'd been so smug and full of herself. Well, fine, she deserved this. Hopefully he'd get it over with quickly. "What is it, Lane?" she demanded as they walked through the parking lot. "What's up?"

His mouth twisted to one side. "Well, I know you girls have heard a little about the Worthington speech."

"Uh-huh." She barely nodded.

"Well, we might joke about it and stuff, but we do take it seriously. Not everyone, but a lot of us do. I mean, maybe the whole non-dating thing goes a little far, but there are other—"

"You know, I hadn't really planned to date," she said suddenly.

"Huh?"

"Before the, um—" She stopped herself from saying DG. "Before some of us girls got all into this homecoming dance, I was determined not to date."

"Really?" He gave her a dubious look.

She held up her hand like a pledge. "Honestly. I even told my parents I wasn't going to date until college." Now she was embarrassed. Why was she going on like this? Why should he care? "But the girls were so gung-ho about this dance . . . I guess I kinda caved." She made a nervous smile. "If you want to bow out of this dance, I'll understand completely. No problem."

He frowned. "You wouldn't be mad?"

She firmly shook her head. "Well, to be honest, I'd be a little disappointed, but I would understand. It might just be for the best." As she said this, she knew it was true. As much as she'd gotten caught up in the DG, she'd felt uneasy about it. There'd been lots of times when she'd considered putting on the brakes and leaping for safety. Maybe this was her chance.

His dark eyes twinkled as a smile crept onto his lips. "Well, that wasn't what I was going to say, Cassidy. But it's kind of good to hear that. I'm glad you're not taking this date too seriously."

Now she wasn't sure whether to be relieved or insulted. What exactly was he saying, anyway?

"What I wanted to tell you is that some of the other guys are kinda concerned. We don't want to fail Worthington's challenge."

"Oh . . . yeah, I get that." She was standing by her car now, twisting the strap of her bag around and around. "Like I said, I'll understand if you want to forget about going to homecoming with me. That's fine." *Just get it over with*, she was thinking impatiently. *Come on!*

"Kent and Harris were talking to me after soccer," he continued in a rambling sort of way. "Kent is kind of into Abby, and I know he's thinking about asking her to the dance, but he wants to make sure she knows he's not looking for a girlfriend." Lane sighed as if he was uncomfortable having this conversation. "That's kind of how we all feel."

Cassidy just laughed. "Well, don't worry, Lane. I'm not looking for a boyfriend either. I just thought it would be fun to go to the dance."

Once again he looked relieved. "That's great."

"I can't speak for the other girls. But I think they were

mostly wanting to go to the dance and have fun, you know? I don't think anyone plans on getting really serious."

"Cool. I'll let the guys know." He looked like he was about to leave.

"Do you think they're going to ask the girls to the dance?" she asked before he could go.

He shrugged. "Maybe."

After they said good-bye, she got into the car and immediately texted the rest of the DG with the good news. Although she couldn't promise anything, she did want them to know that some progress was being made. She also wanted them to know that she'd had something to do with it. Especially Devon, since she sometimes acted like Cassidy was the DG freeloader.

As Cassidy drove home she felt torn. On one hand, she was glad that Lane hadn't broken their date, but on the other hand, she was surprised at how she'd felt a smidgeon of relief to think it could be the end of the Dating Games. Where had that come from? Maybe she knew—maybe she'd just been pretending to be this oblivious. The truth was, Cassidy had been struggling with the spiritual part of her life lately. As badly as she wanted to be a strong Christian and to have an influence on her friends, it seemed she was handling everything completely backwards. Instead of loving her friends, she was often judging them or lecturing them. Just admitting this to herself right now felt lousy.

She thought back to last summer when she'd attended a leadership retreat with some of the youth group from her church. It had been an "invitation only" camp, and she'd felt truly honored to be chosen. The purpose of the camp had been to call the teens to a higher level of commitment. The main focus had been on getting to know God better in order to make God better known among their peers at school. But something they'd talked about a lot was developing their spiritual hearing. They'd been encouraged to tune in to God's "still, small voice." As Cassidy parked her car in the driveway, she felt like she was failing at that.

For starters, what if God had been telling her not to date, but she wasn't listening? After all, Cassidy had given up on dating last year, and now she was in this stupid club. What if she'd allowed God's still, small voice to be drowned out by the likes of Devon Fremont? Just the thought of this was extremely unsettling. It made Cassidy feel like a hypocrite. Not just for ignoring God but also for the way she'd put on the appearance of being so spiritual in front of her friends. What was wrong with her?

Her parents weren't home yet or Cassidy might've asked her mom for some advice. Despite being a mom, she could dish out some pretty good counsel at times. Instead, Cassidy decided to call her favorite youth leader from church.

"I hope I'm not bothering you," she told Julia, "but I need to talk to someone."

"No problem," Julia assured her. "What's going on?"

Without divulging the Dating Games club, she explained how she and four friends were trying to get dates to go to the homecoming dance.

"Good for you," Julia said cheerfully. "That sounds like fun."

"Except that I'd kind of decided not to date," Cassidy confessed. "I mean, last spring I read this book about how dating really messes some people up, so I thought I shouldn't date."

"Oh . . . ?"

"So now I'm feeling kinda guilty, you know? Like maybe I've blown it and I should just cancel my date to the dance."

"Hmmm."

"Do you think I should cancel?"

"Well, you said you decided not to date. Was God the reason you made that decision, Cass? Did you feel like it was something God had directed you to do?"

She thought about this. She wanted to be honest—with herself and Julia. And with God. "It didn't really seem like God. Mostly it was because of the book I read. It just seemed like a good idea." She sighed. "Maybe it was my way to have a good excuse for not dating—I mean, if I never got asked out."

Julia chuckled.

"But it seemed sensible at the time, and I'd planned to stick with it."

"Uh-huh."

"Then I kinda let myself get pulled in with these girls, and the next thing I knew I was planning to go on this date."

"Are these girls your friends?"

"Yeah, sure. For the most part. I mean, there's one girl I don't get along with that well, but I'm trying to be nice to her. She's Emma's friend and she used to go to church, but she's changed a lot since those days. Still, I guess I was hoping I might be a witness to her. And to the others too."

"Cassidy, that's great!"

"Yeah . . . I guess so. But what about this whole dating thing? Do you think I'm blowing it by going on a date? Have I compromised?"

"I think you need to ask God those questions. For sure, if God tells you not to date, then you better listen and obey. But sometimes we run ahead of God and we start making up rules for ourselves. Rules that aren't really from God. It's almost like we think we can impress God, which is totally ridiculous. The next thing we know we're caught up in legalism—you know, where you make a rule and think that God is going to be pleased with you for keeping it. That's not how he works. That's how religion works. But God doesn't want us to be religious. He wants us to have a relationship with him. Not a bunch of rules."

"Yeah. I get that."

"It all comes back down to listening to him. Are you spending time with God? Reading your Bible and praying every day?"

"I'm trying to."

"Good. That's the best way to get God's direction. Then you need to listen to your own heart too, Cassidy. Like how about the guy you're going to the dance with—is he a *good* guy?"

"Yeah. Absolutely." She even told Julia about how Lane was committed to the guys' code of honor. "Some of the other guys are like that too."

"That's cool. I think it would be awesome for Christian kids to go on a group date to have a good time together. What a great example for others."

"You think it's okay then?"

Julia chuckled. "Sorry, Cass, that's not how it works. You can't call me and ask for my permission or my blessing and run off without thinking for yourself. I can give you advice, but you have to go to God for the specific answers. Listen to him and listen to your heart."

Cassidy knew Julia was right, but it would be so much easier if she would just tell her what to do.

"Here's another bit of advice," Julia said. "When I'm asking God for direction in my own life, I do a peace inventory before I make a decision."

"Piece of what?" Cassidy asked.

"You know, like the peace that passes understanding. The peace that rules in your heart when you're right with God."

"Oh, yeah."

"If I don't get a sense of peace about something I'm about to do, I take that as God telling me no, or that I need to wait. And believe me, I've ignored it a couple of times, and I've been pretty sorry later."

"Yeah, I'm sure I've done that too."

"Don't forget that following God is a one day at a time thing, Cassidy. Just because God gives you a green light to go on this date doesn't mean that he's telling you to get into dating in a big way. Remember too that guys are part of the equation. Never go out with a guy you don't trust—or one you don't have peace about. To be honest, I can think of a lot of good reasons that some girls don't date at all. For one thing, dating can really derail a relationship with God."

"Okay, now you're making me confused again."

Julia laughed. "Sorry. Back to square one. It's up to you to figure this stuff out. No one else can tell you what to do. Well, that is, unless your parents are opposed to dating. I know some girls with parents like that. And I respect them for it."

"No, my parents are okay."

"Well, I'm sure God will make it clear to you, Cassidy."

"Right now it feels as clear as mud."

Julia promised to pray for Cassidy and her friends as well. "Keep me posted on how it turns out," she said before they hung up.

Cassidy put her phone away, then bowed her head. She was determined to do this God's way.

"Please, God, show me what you want me to do in regard to dating," she said slowly. "Help me to tune my ears to your still, small voice." She sat quietly for a while, trying to listen. Soon she felt a nudge—not an answer to her prayer, but as if she should be praying for the other girls in the DG. Wanting to be obedient to that quiet voice, she began to pray for each of them—one by one and by name. As she prayed, she realized that she really cared about all of them. Even Devon. She even took time to pray for the guys that the girls were trying to entice as dates. She asked God to help them to keep their code of honor—even if it meant no one went to the dance in the end. Really, what did it matter if they all stayed home?

When she finally said amen, she realized she did have a sense of peace. The weird thing was that she felt that she would be at peace whether or not she went to the homecoming dance. Because now, more than ever, she felt a sense of mission—as if God was calling her to something more important than just going on a date and attending a dance. She wasn't sure quite how she would do it, and she suspected she'd been going about everything all wrong previously—especially the way she'd treated her friends—but from here on out she wanted to do a better job of making God known to her friends. She knew that meant she would have to become a better friend first.

On Friday morning, Bryn knew it was time to pull out all the stops. Her goal was to secure a date to the dance before the school day ended. Whether it was with Jason or Harris made little difference to her. In fact, she was just about fed up with these flaky boys. One minute they were shamelessly flirting with her, and the next she heard rumors that they were fretting about letting old Worthington down. Well, this was high school, and Devon was right—it was supposed to be a time for fun. And she was ready for the fun to begin.

To this end, she had taken extra time to put herself together perfectly this morning. Every golden hair was in place, and she made sure to wear an outfit that showed off her best boy-attracting assets. Plus, she had a plan. She would play Jason against Harris, and if she was lucky, she would manage to get one of those boys jealous enough to do something. At least she hoped so. The dance was just a week away, and this was getting ridiculous. Not to mention embarrassing. How was it that the two least likely girls—shy little Emma and Goody-Two-Shoes Cassidy—had both been asked to the dance? Meanwhile Bryn, Abby, and Devon were still standing on the sidelines. It was maddening.

"What's up with you?" Abby asked as Bryn came striding through the locker bay toward her. "You look like you're on the warpath or something."

Bryn nodded. "You got that right."

"Uh-oh. Who crossed you?"

"Mr. Worthington," Bryn said quietly.

"Huh?" Abby looked around like she expected to see Mr. Worthington approaching.

"He's totally brainwashed the boys," Bryn whispered. "It's just not fair. Today I plan to put an end to this no-dating nonsense."

Abby laughed. "Hey, let me know when it's going down. I so don't want to miss this."

"High noon," Bryn told her. "And I'm bringing in the big guns."

Abby's brown eyes got bigger.

Bryn laughed. "Sorry. My dad was watching an old John Wayne flick last night."

"What are you going to do?"

"Wait and see," Bryn told her. "Watch and learn." Holding her head high, Bryn waved to her friend and strutted off. Her goal was to imitate the persona of a confident, carefree celebrity. She knew this charade was bordering on the ridiculous, but she just couldn't help herself. She'd cast herself into this role, and she was determined to play it out.

For the whole morning she kept up her bold act of flirtatious self-assurance, and strangely enough, it seemed people were buying it. At least they were looking at her differently. And it felt pretty good. Maybe she should act like this all the time.

As fourth period ended, she wondered if she could actually pull this thing off. At the same time she didn't really care, though—because she was having fun. As she was heading to the cafeteria, she spotted Harris coming out of the math department. "Hey, Harris," she said in a flirty tone. "What's up?"

He grinned as if he was pleased to see her. "Not much."

She tossed a length of hair over her shoulder and showered him with her most sparkly smile as she pointed to his chest. "I sure like that shirt on you. Great color."

"Thanks." His eyes lit up as he looked at her. "Something about you seems different. I mean good different."

"Thanks!"

Harris continued walking with her, making small talk, and she continued to flirt, until finally they were entering the cafeteria together. Perfect!

As they went inside she dissolved her smile. "I just feel so bad about something. I probably shouldn't even mention it, though."

"Bad?" He looked confused. "About what?"

"Well . . ." She stopped walking and turned to look at him. "I'd just really hoped that you were going to ask me to the homecoming dance. It would've been so fun to go with you." She sighed. "But now you're too late."

He looked even more confused. "Too late?"

She shrugged. "Oh, it's okay. I'm sure you'll still have a good time. I know I will. Maybe someday . . ."

"But I—uh—I mean . . . I wasn't even sure if I was going to the dance."

She waved her hand dismissively. "Oh, never mind about it. I saw you today and I thought . . . well, I just wish things had worked out differently between us." She smiled. "You know?"

He looked completely bewildered. "But I thought you were trying to set me up with Devon. Weren't you—"

"It's okay," she assured him. "I understand." Right then she spotted Jason entering the cafeteria. The timing couldn't have been better.

"But if you still want to—"

"Hey, Jason," she called out, waving.

"Hey," he said as he joined them. "What's up?"

"Not much." She put a hand on Harris's shoulder. "I was just telling Harris how I would've loved to have gone to the homecoming dance."

Jason looked slightly confused now.

"But you *boys*." She shook her head in a dismal way. "I just didn't realize how Worthington has some of you under his thumb. Really, it's kinda cute how loyal to him you are." She gave them an impish smile. "Boring, yes, but it is sweet. And it's helped me to realize I need to find a different kind of guy." She reached over and stroked Jason's cheek. "Too bad, huh?" She turned to walk away.

"Wait." It was Harris calling out to her.

She turned back, giving him an innocent look. "What?"

He hurried over to her. "I'm not under Worthington's thumb. I'd be glad to take you to the dance, Bryn."

"Really?" She gave him a full-eyed look of adoration, like she'd hooked this fish and planned to reel him in.

"Yeah. Do you want to go with me?"

Jason came over now. "Wait a minute," he said. "I thought Bryn was going to go to the dance with me. That's what Abby has been leading me to believe."

She tilted her head to one side. "If that's what you thought, I wonder why you didn't ask me sooner. I just assumed it was because you were letting Worthington call the shots."

"Jason doesn't care about the Worthington speech," Harris said quickly. "Everyone knows that."

Bryn frowned. "Oh?"

"Yeah." Harris glanced at Jason as if he was unsure. "He was holding out for Amanda."

"That's a lie!" Jason shot back at him.

Harris held his hands up. "Hey, don't shoot the messenger. That's what I heard."

"Well, it's a lie." Jason grabbed Harris by a shoulder.

"Easy, boys." Bryn put a hand between them. "Let's not make a scene, okay?"

"Just don't go shooting your mouth off about things you don't understand," Jason said to Harris.

Bryn could tell by Harris's eyes that he was a little scared. Jason was several inches and a lot of pounds bigger. Bryn's heart softened toward Harris, and although she knew Devon would be furious, she decided she didn't care. She pointed at Harris. "Well, since you asked first, I will be happy to go to the dance with you."

Harris blinked in surprise. "Cool."

Jason's eyes narrowed, and it was obvious he was seething.

Pretending to be completely at ease, she placed a hand on his shoulder. "If you're looking for a date for the dance, why don't you talk to Devon?" she said gently. "I think you two could really hit it off."

"Maybe I'll do that," he said gruffly.

Bryn turned back to Harris now. "I guess we can work out the details later. But just so you know, I'm looking forward to it." She ran her hand down his arm as she gave him her most effervescent smile. He looked like he was about ready to melt. Perfect. She walked away, going over to the regular table where her DG friends were watching with dropped jaws.

"What did you just do?" Devon demanded.

Abby nodded to the chair next to her. "You said you were having a showdown at lunch today, but I thought you were kidding."

"Harris looked totally smitten," Emma said. "Are you going to the dance with him?"

"What about Jason?" Cassidy asked. "I thought you were supposed to be going with him."

"Remember, these are the Dating *Games*," Bryn said. "And the game plan has just changed." She pointed at Devon. "FYI, I think Jason is going to ask you to the dance."

Devon looked slightly flustered but not entirely unhappy.

"What did you do?" Emma asked. "What did you say?"

Bryn shrugged as she sat down, removing a lunch sack from her oversized bag. "I just used my head and my natural assets."

The girls laughed.

"Seriously, I thought it all through," she told them as she pulled out an apple. "I turned on the charm and turned up the heat, and voilà, it all fell into place."

"But with Harris?" Devon shook her head. "Why?"

"The way I saw it, it was like I had to break open this dam—the Worthington dam—and I went for the weakest link. Turned out that was Harris." She peered at Devon. "Come on, you told us before that you think Jason is hot.

Why don't you do like I did? Use your wits and your good looks and nail a date with the boy." Bryn laughed. "It's not that difficult. Especially since I got him warmed up for you."

"What about me?" Abby asked in a meek voice.

Bryn grinned at her. "Don't worry. Now that I got Harris on board, it will be a cinch to get Kent. Trust me, before this day is over, you'll have a date for the dance."

"With Kent?" Abby looked uneasy.

Bryn shrugged. "Does it really matter? I mean, I thought I wanted to go with Jason, but I'm settling for Harris. The point was that we wanted to go to the dance, right? Maybe we shouldn't be too picky about who's taking us."

Abby pursed her lips like she was considering this.

"I'll do my best," Bryn promised. She pulled a paperback from her bag. "If you'll excuse me, I need to get some reading done before English."

It was hard to concentrate on *A Farewell to Arms* now, but at least it provided a good distraction from answering questions from her friends. Bryn felt exhausted from her role-playing stint. Sure, it had been fun, but it was not an act she could keep up indefinitely.

However, as the day progressed, she was aware of the promise she'd made to Abby. Somehow she had to get Kent on board. To do this, she realized she would need help—and Harris would be her man.

"Hey, Harris," she said, catching up with him after the final bell rang. "Can we talk?"

He looked slightly alarmed. "You're not going to dump me already, are you?"

She laughed as she linked her arm into his. "Not at all."

He looked relieved. "What do you want to talk about?"

"I need your help," she said in the same tone she used on her dad when she wanted something.

"What can I do for you?" He seemed to square his shoulders and stand taller.

She smiled. "You're good friends with Kent, right?"

"Yeah. Absolutely."

"Well, Abby is my best friend, and it looks like she could be left out of going to the dance. Honestly, I don't see how I could possibly have a good time if my best friend wasn't there. You know?"

He nodded eagerly. "You want me to work on Kent?"

"Could you?"

"You bet. He owes me a favor anyway."

She beamed at him. "Thanks so much, Harris. I'm so glad we got this all worked out. What if I'd had to go to the dance with a different guy?"

"That would've been a shame." He explained that they had an away soccer game after school and he needed to hurry to catch the bus. "But I will get Kent on board. Count on it."

"Let me know." She held up her phone.

"You got it."

Okay, so she hadn't quite nailed it for Abby yet. Hadn't she promised by the end of the day? Well, this day wasn't over. As Bryn walked to her locker, she wondered if going to the dance was really worth this much effort. Oh, it would be fun and all. But if dating required so much time and energy, was it worth it? As she rounded a corner, she spied a familiar redhead—Devon—cozying up to Jason. For a moment, Bryn felt slightly jealous. After all, she was the one who was supposed to be going to the dance with Jason. But to be fair, she'd been the one who'd changed the game plan, so she couldn't complain. Still, Jason was awfully good looking. It irked her to see Devon so obviously flirting with him. That could've been Bryn.

Bryn held her head high as she sauntered past the two of them. She hoped that Jason would see her—and that he'd regret that he hadn't acted sooner. Really, it was his loss.

She stopped by the restroom on her way, and before she emerged from the stall some senior girls came in. They were clustered at the sinks, probably primping, as they talked. "It figures Jason would be attracted to a girl like *that*," a voice that sounded like Amanda was saying. "He's been looking for a lowlife, and unless I'm mistaken, that redhead is just the ticket."

"Ooh, sounds like sour grapes to me," another girl said.

"It's *not* sour grapes," Amanda retorted. "I've already told you, I'm finished with him. That guy has one thing on his mind, and trust me, it's not his brain that's doing the thinking."

They all laughed.

"He thinks girls are nothing more than sex objects," Amanda continued. "Like we were put here on this earth simply to make him happy. Seriously, he is the most selfish guy on the planet."

"Then how did you stay with him for so long?" a girl asked.

"Believe me, it wasn't easy. That new girl—that skanky little redhead—well, she can have him. They probably deserve each other."

Amanda and her friends were laughing as Bryn got ready to emerge from the stall, preparing herself to defend Devon. But before she could think of anything to say, it was obvious that the senior girls were leaving. Besides, Bryn wondered as she washed her hands, what would she say? How well did she really know Devon? For all she knew, Devon could be exactly as Amanda had said.

After all, Bryn's first impression of Devon had been that she was boy crazy. And everyone knew about first impressions—they were lasting. Besides that, Devon was the one who'd suggested their club in the first place. She was the one who was so hot to date. Of course, thinking about this just filled Bryn with more questions. If Devon really was that kind of girl, why had they allowed her to take the lead in creating the Dating Games club? Were they going to regret this later?

Just as Bryn reached her locker, she received a text from Harris. The soccer guys were on the bus heading across town, and it sounded like Harris had already gotten Kent to agree to take Abby to the dance. So it was all set. No time to look back. She didn't want to anyway. She'd set out to accomplish certain goals today, and it appeared that she'd done exactly that. Instead of questioning herself and their club, she should be patting herself on the back!

I could hardly believe it," Abby told Bryn when she called on Saturday morning. "Just when I was about to give up on Kent last night—after you'd gotten my hopes up—he finally came through."

"I told you he would."

"Maybe . . . but to be honest it was a little disappointing." Abby kicked off her Nikes and peeled off her sweaty socks. She'd run five miles with her dad this morning and was yearning for a good long shower right now.

"Disappointing? What do you mean?"

"I mean he texted me what felt like a really cautious invitation to the dance."

"Cautious? How so?"

Abby tried to remember the exact message, but it was kind of muddled in her mind now. "Oh, I don't know exactly. It just seemed like he was trying to make it perfectly clear that we were only going together as *friends*."

"Well, that's okay. Isn't it?"

"Yeah, I guess. But after all we've been through with the DG and everyone putting so much effort into this thing . . . well, it was kind of anticlimactic."

Bryn laughed. "Don't be silly. At least you're going to the dance, Abby. Isn't that something to celebrate? I was so worried you'd be left out."

"Speaking of left out . . . What about Devon?" Abby struggled out of her T-shirt as she held onto her phone.

"What about her?" Bryn's voice turned flat.

"Well, she hasn't been asked yet."

"I know."

"You got her text this morning, didn't you? After I sent mine announcing that I was officially going?"

"Yeah, I got it." Bryn sounded slightly agitated now.

Of course, this only stirred up Abby's curiosity. Suddenly her urge to get into the shower was much less pressing. She sat down on her bed. "So what's up with Devon? And why do you sound irritated at her?"

"Didn't you *read* the text?" Bryn demanded.

"Yeah. Well, I read it pretty fast. I was just about ready to go running with Dad and—"

"Did you miss the part where Devon was pulling the plug on our homecoming dates?"

"Huh?" Abby held her phone out, wishing she could read the message more carefully this time.

"Yes, Devon snarkily reminded us of the 'no girl left behind' rule. Remember that rule?"

"Oh . . ." Abby flopped back on her bed and groaned. "So after everything we've gone through, Devon thinks we should all cancel just because she doesn't have a date to homecoming?"

"Uh-huh. That pretty much describes it."

"Man, that bites."

"Tell me about it. I put a lot of work into this project."

"It's not our fault she hasn't been asked out," Abby said.

"Well, maybe. But I happen to know she's blaming me."

"Huh?" Abby sat up.

"Yeah. She called me a little while ago saying that if I hadn't hit on Harris, she would be going with him."

"Right . . . maybe in her dreams." Abby sighed. "What are we going to do?"

"We're getting her a date." Bryn said this with such determination that it sounded like a done deal.

"Have you had any luck with Jason?"

"No, but she probably deserves him," Bryn said sharply.

"What's that supposed to mean?"

"I mean, from what I hear, Jason isn't exactly a nice guy."

"What did you hear?" Abby didn't really like gossip, at least not when it was about her friends. But when it was about someone else . . . well, her curiosity sometimes got the best of her. Abby was all ears as Bryn jumped right into a story about overhearing Amanda and her friends talking about Jason in the restroom.

"I don't see any reason why Amanda would lie—at least not to her friends," Bryn continued. "She made it sound like Jason would be the last guy at Northwood to take the Worthington challenge seriously. Like Jason was after one thing and one thing only when it came to girls. I think those were her exact words."

"Did you tell Devon this?"

"Are you kidding?"

"But what about the DG rules?" Abby reminded her. "We're supposed to be loyal to each other. Remember?"

"Yeah, but how loyal is it for Devon to tell us we can't go to homecoming? Or to blame me for her failure to get a date?"

"Good point. But still . . ." Abby didn't like Devon that much. Certainly not as much as she liked the other girls in the club. Even so, she'd always had a strong sense of fairness. In her mind, a commitment was a commitment.

"Anyway, it seems the only thing to do is find Devon a date," Bryn said.

"Yes, obviously. But who can we get? The dance is less than a week away."

"I know. And I found the perfect guy for her." Bryn giggled.

"Who?"

"Darrell Zuckerman."

"Darrell Zuckerman?" Abby didn't like to label people, but anyone else in school would call Darrell Zuckerman a geek. Maybe even a super geek since he seemed to make the most of his status by dressing and acting as weird as possible. Besides being a geek, he was an atheist, which was ironic since Northwood Academy was considered a Christian school. But Darrell obviously wasn't there by choice, and he never seemed to mind who knew this. He wasn't just a geek, he was an obnoxious, outspoken, opinionated geek. Abby had him in trigonometry, and his attitude regarding his superior math skills got old quick.

"He's my lab partner in chemistry," Bryn explained. "I know most people don't understand him, but we actually get along pretty well. He likes me. And I like him."

"Maybe *you* should go to the dance with him," Abby teased. "And leave Harris for Devon."

"Abby!"

"Kidding."

"Anyway, I took the liberty of texting him this morning—right after Devon texted me—and then he called and we talked it all through, and he is willing to take her."

"He's willing?" Abby laughed. "Like it's a big imposition for someone like Darrell to take someone like Devon?"

"Hey, Darrell might be a geek, but he's not stupid."

"I wasn't saying he was. I just thought he might appreciate having a pretty girl like Devon on his arm. You know? Might elevate his status in geekdom."

"Well, as it turns out, you're right." Bryn laughed. "Once I convinced him this wasn't a prank, he agreed. He wants to take her."

"What did Devon say?"

"Devon doesn't know yet."

"Oh, I can't wait to hear her reaction." Suddenly Abby felt sorry for Darrell. "Does she even know Darrell?"

"I'm not sure. I think you'll have the opportunity to hear her reaction, though. I've called a meeting for today. If you ever checked your phone, you'd know this. Anyway, can you be at Costello's by 11:00? I already got confirmation from everyone else."

"I guess so, but I still need to grab a shower. You could've given me more notice."

"I tried. Tell me, once again, why you don't take your phone with you when you go running?"

"When I'm with my dad? What for?" Abby was tugging off her shorts now.

"Never mind. See you at 11:00. I'll order you a mocha."

Abby hurried to shower and dress, then hopped on her bike and headed toward town. Fortunately, her house was less than a mile from Costello's, but by the time she went into the coffee shop, her friends were already seated.

"Sorry," she said breathlessly as she took a chair. "Did you guys start without me?"

Bryn shook her head and passed a coffee mug toward Abby. "Nope. We wanted everyone here and accounted for."

"I know why you called the meeting," Devon said with an unhappy expression. "You're mad at me for putting the kibosh on the dance, but if you remember, we all agreed to—"

"No, that's not it," Bryn interrupted. "I called this meeting because I have good news."

"Good news?" Devon's thin brows arched.

"You have a date for the dance."

"Really?" Devon smiled. "Jason came through? But he hasn't even—"

"Not Jason," Bryn said quickly.

Devon's smile faded. "Who then?"

"A good friend of mine," Bryn began. "He's my lab partner in chemistry. Very smart. I honestly don't know what I'd do without him. And fortunately for us, he didn't even go to Mr. Worthington's little talk. He's what you'd call an independent thinker."

Devon looked interested. "I like that."

"Who is it?" Emma asked, and Abby suppressed the urge to giggle.

"It's Darrell Zuckerman." Bryn seemed to be giving the other girls a warning look. "As we agreed on at our very first meeting, it doesn't matter so much who we date since these are just the Dating Games and we're all beginners. I think Darrell will be a perfect date for Devon."

Cassidy looked like she was trying not to laugh as she

nodded eagerly. "Yeah, I think so too. Darrell should be a really interesting date for you, Devon."

"What does he *look* like?" Devon asked with a worried expression. "Have I ever even met him?"

"Oh, you've probably seen him around," Bryn assured her. "He's got brown hair, average height—"

"Very solidly built," Abby interjected. "I'm surprised he doesn't go out for football." Well, except that he probably didn't have an athletic bone in his body and his "solidness" was probably the result of too many pizzas and video games, but she was not going there.

"What if I don't like him?" Devon said with a creased brow.

Bryn shrugged. "I guess we can't help that. But since we got you a date for the dance, you can't claim that we left you out, right?"

"But what if I don't want to—"

"Remember what you told us," Emma said. "As long as we all had dates, it—"

"But that was when I thought Harris was taking me . . . or Jason."

"Has Jason made any moves in your direction?" Cassidy asked pointedly.

"Not exactly." Devon looked at Bryn. "But you were working on him for me. You said it looked hopeful."

"I thought it did." Bryn sighed. "But really, maybe it's for the best, Devon. From what I hear Jason isn't such a great catch. Personally, I'm glad not to be going to the dance with him."

"What do you mean he's not a good catch?" Devon demanded.

Bryn grimaced, and Abby decided to jump in, retelling what Bryn had told her. "It sounds like both of you dodged a bullet by not going out with him," she said. "Be thankful."

"I think you're just making that up." Devon glared at Bryn.

"I swear it's true," Bryn assured her. "Almost exactly like Abby just told you. I'm sure that's why Amanda broke up with him. She sounded fed up."

"Well, maybe Amanda was jerking you around because she wants Jason back."

"Amanda had no idea I was listening."

"Even so." Devon glared at her and the others. "Whoever this Darrell person is, I'm almost certain that I'm not going to like him. This is just your way of making sure you all go to the dance even if I'm dateless. It's just not fair." She hit the table with her fist, making their coffee cups jitter.

Suddenly they were all talking at once, arguing over what was and wasn't fair, who had done what and who hadn't. Finally, after Abby noticed some of the other coffee patrons giving them looks of irritation, she made an attempt to bring the group to order. "I say we should vote on it," she told everyone. "All in favor of Devon going to the dance with Darrell, raise their hands." Four hands shot up, and Devon just rolled her eyes.

"You obviously have the right to refuse to go with him," Bryn told Devon. "But you have to admit that we didn't let you down by not getting you a date."

"A loser date." Devon narrowed her eyes at Bryn. "How would you like to be stuck with him?"

Bryn gave Devon the slightly superior look she could sometimes pull off. "I would make the best of it," she declared, "for the sake of my friends—and for Darrell."

"I believe that," Abby confirmed. "I've known Bryn for years and that's how she is."

"Fine." Devon stood up. "I'll consider going with Darrell what's-his-name. But not until I see him first. And just for the record, I am not happy about this."

After she left, the four girls burst into giggles. "You know she'll never go with him," Cassidy said finally.

"Maybe she'd like him if she got to know him," Bryn said wistfully. "I like him."

"Enough to go to the dance with him?" Emma asked.

Bryn seemed to consider this. "Maybe . . . maybe I would."

"Well, if Devon thinks she can switch dates on you, she probably will," Abby warned. "You better be prepared for it."

"Yeah, getting Darrell for Devon is kind of a low blow," Emma said.

"I happen to like Darrell," Cassidy interjected. "I mean, he's weird, but he's nice. And he's über-smart."

"Maybe you should go with him," Emma told her. "Let Devon have Lane."

Cassidy frowned. "I don't know . . . I doubt Lane would be that into Devon."

"Well, I'm sorry she's not being more cooperative," Bryn said. "I only set her up with Darrell for you guys. I know how much everyone was looking forward to the dance. I didn't want Devon to ruin it for us."

"I think you saved the day," Abby told Bryn. She looked at the others. "Don't you guys agree?" Emma and Cassidy nodded. "Speaking of the dance, my mom wants to go shoe shopping with me. I better get moving."

"Before you leave," Cassidy said quickly, "I wanted to say something. I'd meant to say it while Devon was here."

"What's wrong?" Emma asked.

"Nothing's wrong," Cassidy said. "I just wanted to apologize to you guys. I know I've been kind of grumpy and negative lately, and I don't really like acting that way. I mean . . . it's not very Christlike. And I'm sorry."

Everyone at the table was quiet now, as if waiting for her to continue.

She smiled. "I just want to try to be more positive, you know. I want to work harder at being a better friend."

"That's cool," Abby said, and the others echoed her, but it was obvious they were all a little uncomfortable with her unexpected declaration. Cassidy could be like that, and you never really knew where she was going with something.

"Don't worry," Cassidy said, "it's not like I'm going to start preaching at you." She laughed. "Well, I'll try not to anyway. But I did have an idea for the homecoming dance. Actually, it was my mom's idea, but I think it's a good one." She reminded them of how they'd kind of wrangled the guys into taking them and how there were expenses involved, including a nice meal somewhere. "How about if we provide dinner? I'm willing to host it at my house," she told them. "I thought each of us could bring one dish. You know, like someone brings a salad and someone brings a—"

"Like a potluck?" Bryn frowned.

"No, like a really elegant dinner. We'll plan the menu. My mom said we can have it in the dining room and use her good china and have candles and fresh flowers and the works. I'll take care of all that."

"I think that sounds nice," Emma said.

"I do too," Abby agreed. "It'll take some pressure off the guys' wallets too."

"Let's vote," Bryn said. Naturally, it was unanimous.

As Abby hopped on her bike and headed for home, she felt inexplicably hopeful about their upcoming date. Oh, sure, Devon might not be too happy with the new arrangements, but at least she couldn't claim that they'd left her behind. And who knew, maybe she'd even like Darrell. Although Abby doubted it. Devon seemed a little too superficial to enjoy a date with someone as quirky as Darrell Zuckerman.

Instead of worrying about that, Abby thought about Kent. In a way it was a relief that he'd made it clear that he only wanted to go out with her as a friend. After all, she wasn't ready for a hot and heavy relationship. At least she could reassure her dad that nothing would get out of hand on her first date, and she could say that honestly. This was all working out much better than she could have hoped for. Now if she could just find a really cool pair of shoes today!

As soon as she came into the house, Emma knew that something was wrong. Mom was on the phone, but the expression on her face was extremely somber. Emma's immediate thoughts went to Edward. Had something happened to him at college?

"Yes," Mom said sadly. "But it's up to you whether or not you should come home, Edward. Don't do anything to jeopardize your classes." She glanced at Emma. "He wouldn't want that."

Emma frowned. "Who?" she whispered.

Mom held up her hand. "Well, Emma's here now," she said. "I need to tell her what's happened." She told Edward she loved him and said good-bye, then turned to Emma with tears in her eyes. "It's your grandpa," she said solemnly.

"What?" Emma demanded. "Is he sick again?"

"He suffered a heart attack this morning. He died before the ambulance even got there."

Emma felt her world spinning. "Grandpa?" she cried. "Grandpa is dead?"

Mom just nodded, reaching for Emma. She hugged her tightly.

"But I was supposed to go over there this week," Emma said through sobs. "To help him sort out the photos." The tears started coming so fast she couldn't even talk. Grandpa was gone—and she hadn't even gone over there like she'd promised. Now it was too late.

Mom was stroking her hair. "Grandpa's in a better place," she said quietly. "You know that."

Emma stepped back and stared at Mom's tear-streaked face. "But I let him down." She choked out the words. "I didn't go like I said I would."

"Grandpa would understand," Mom said.

"No." Emma shook her head. "I let him down."

The phone rang, and while Mom answered it, Emma dashed to her room and let the tears flow freely. Guilt and sadness washed over her, and she couldn't believe she would never see him again. Through it all—Dad leaving them and everything else—Grandpa had always been there for her. But where had she been when he needed her? Off trying to connive a stupid date for a ridiculous dance. Oh, if only she'd never heard of the Dating Games club. Why had she allowed that horrible club to distract her from something that really mattered? Like spending time with Grandpa . . . before it was too late. How could she ever forgive herself? One thing she knew for certain—she was not going to the dance now. No way!

• • • • •

By Monday, Emma's mood had not improved much. She still felt guilty for not spending time with her grandpa before his death, and she still missed him deeply. Why did a person have to lose someone before they fully appreciated them? Afterwards, it was too late.

"I'm sorry about your grandfather," Cassidy told Emma as they met on the way to the English department. "I heard about it at church yesterday. I know he was an elder in the church. My dad was saying what a great guy he was and how much he'll be missed."

Emma nodded sadly. "Yeah, he was . . . and he will be."

Cassidy put her arm around Emma, pulling her into a comforting hug. "Well, if you need to talk or anything, I'm here."

"Thanks." Emma blinked back tears. As they went to their classes, Emma compared Cassidy's words to Devon's. Oh, Devon had been sorry, of course, but she'd also been focused on Jason, and she'd seemed obsessed with her plan for getting him to take her to the dance. Emma had almost felt like Devon had brushed her off. When Emma had mentioned that she might not go to the dance, Devon had acted like that was unthinkable.

"Just give yourself some time," she'd said casually. "You'll get over it by then."

Emma hadn't responded to that, but she knew Devon was wrong. She even questioned what kind of a friend Devon truly was. It was hard enough losing her grandpa, but perhaps she was losing her best friend too.

By lunchtime, Emma had made up her mind. She was going to seek out Isaac and explain her need to cancel their date. Hopefully he would understand. If he was determined to go to the dance, maybe he could take Devon instead of her. That might just make everyone happy.

She found Isaac coming out of the math department and called out to him. He looked surprised but smiled as he came over to join her. But when he saw her expression, his smile faded. "Hey, what's wrong? You look like you just lost your best friend."

"It's kinda like that," she told him quietly. "Can we talk?"

His fair brows arched, but he nodded and followed her over to a quiet corner. "What's up?"

She explained that her grandpa had died. "I know some people think I'm overreacting, but I just can't help myself." She tried to hold back the tears. "He was really special to me, and I'm so sad . . . I just don't see how I can go to the dance."

Isaac nodded soberly. "I understand."

"I'm sorry." The tears were coming again. She wiped them with her hand. "It's just really hard right now."

Isaac gathered her up in a hug—a sweet, warm hug. "It's okay, Emma. I do understand," he whispered. "My mom died a few years ago, and it was pretty rough on me."

She stepped back and looked at him. "Your mom died?" She wiped her cheeks with the cuff of her hoodie. "I didn't know that."

"Yeah. I was in middle school. She'd had cancer for a long time, so I should've been prepared for it. But I wasn't."

She shook her head. "Oh . . . I'm sorry. I kinda know how you feel."

He peered into her eyes. "Are you sure you don't want to go to the dance, though? I mean, I do understand if you don't. But it might be good for you."

She sighed. "I don't know."

"Well, if you want to think about it, that's fine. And if you decide not to, it won't be a problem. Really."

Emma had liked Isaac from afar for a while, but she was surprised to discover he was this thoughtful up close. "Thanks," she told him. "I appreciate that."

He patted her on the back. "I know it's hard to believe it now," he said in an assuring tone, "but it will get better with time."

She shrugged. "I'm not sure it will." She explained how guilty she felt for not making it over to see her grandpa last week. "I didn't realize I'd never get another chance."

"Oh . . ." He looked concerned. "That's gotta be hard. Was your grandfather a believer? I mean, was he a Christian?"

"Yes." She nodded. "Absolutely."

Isaac brightened. "Then you'll see him again someday, right?"

She sighed. "I guess so."

He looked surprised. "You guess so?"

"Well . . . yeah . . . I mean, sometimes I'm not so sure about all that."

He looked dismayed now. "You don't believe in heaven?"

She thought about it. "Well, I guess I do. I guess I just haven't given it much thought."

"Well, you should," he declared. "Especially in light of losing your grandfather. When my mom died, it was all I had to hold on to—believing that I'd see her again."

"You don't have any doubts?" she questioned.

"Oh, sure, everyone has doubts sometimes. But faith is a gift from God. So I just take my doubts to him."

She looked at Isaac as if seeing him for the first time. "You're quite a guy, you know?"

He laughed. "Well, thanks."

"I had no idea you had so much depth to you."

He made a shy smile. "That's because you didn't really know me."

She smiled back. "I'd like to get to know you . . . I mean, as a friend."

He got a thoughtful look. "Can I ask you a question—about your grandpa?"

"Sure."

"How do you think he feels right now—I mean, if he's thinking about you? Do you think he's angry or hurt that you didn't come to see him?"

She thought hard for a moment, then shook her head. "No. My grandpa wasn't like that. He was really kind and forgiving. And besides, if he's in heaven—which I'm sure he is—he probably has better things to do than worry about me."

Isaac grinned. "That sounds about right."

Emma felt her stomach growling. "You know, I haven't had an appetite for a couple of days, and suddenly I feel hungry."

"That's a good sign," he said, nodding toward the cafeteria. "Let's get some lunch."

As they walked she told him a little about her grandpa, like some of the things she used to do with him and how she would miss him. It was weird, but instead of it making her feel sadder, she felt like the black cloud she'd been under the past few days was starting to thin a little. Maybe there was hope.

Before they parted ways in the cafeteria, she thanked Isaac

once again for encouraging her. "I'll let you know about the dance," she promised. "Maybe I was making a knee-jerk reaction."

"I wonder what your grandpa would want you to do."

"Well, I'll tell you this much, I do think my grandpa would like you," she admitted.

His face lit up. "I'm sure I'd like him too."

She felt lighter as she walked over to the table where her friends were already seated.

"Looks like you changed your mind," Devon said a bit smugly. "You're going to the dance with Isaac after all?"

"Why weren't you going to go to the dance?" Bryn demanded. "I thought it was all set."

"Her grandpa died," Devon explained in a know-it-all tone. "I know it's a bummer, but it's still no reason not to go to the dance."

"It's a reason if Emma says it's a reason," Cassidy countered. "If she's too sad to enjoy the dance, no one should pressure her."

"But you just saw her with Isaac," Devon said. "She was smiling."

"That's because Isaac was being so sweet," Emma told them as she set her bag on a chair. "He's such a nice guy."

"A nice guy who doesn't deserve to be dumped," Devon said.

"No one said anything about dumping anyone," Emma told her.

"I'm sorry about your grandpa," Abby said. "I'd be devastated if my grandpa died. We're really close."

Emma sniffed. "So were we. I miss him so much."

"I'm sorry too," Bryn told her. "I hadn't heard about it. I

know he went to our church, but I missed the service yesterday. I didn't know him, but he seemed like a really nice guy."

Emma nodded. "He was."

"Okay," Devon said with impatience. "If we've all shared our condolences with Emma, does anyone want to hear about me?"

"Oh, I forgot," Bryn said snarkily. "It's all about *you*, right?"

Devon glared at her. "Well, it's no thanks to you, but I thought you might like to know that I do have a date for the homecoming dance. And it's not that geeky Darrell dude either. Eww."

Emma's stomach growled again. "I'd love to stay and hear more," she told Devon, "but I'm starving."

Devon frowned as Emma hurried away. Emma had no interest in hearing about Devon's date for homecoming, so despite being really hungry, Emma decided to take her time getting her lunch and returning to their table. Hopefully Devon would be gone by then.

"Well, I waited for you," Devon said as Emma sat down.

Emma gave her a blasé look that said, *Whatever.*

"Fine," Devon said sharply. "Don't listen if you don't want to." Devon went into a detailed account of how she'd cornered Jason down by the gym this morning. "I looked him right in the eye and I said, 'It's too bad you're not taking me to the homecoming dance.'" She pointed at Bryn. "I learned that line from you."

"What did he say?" Bryn asked with mild interest.

"I could tell he was intrigued. I told him he'd be missing out on a really fun night. And I told him that he wouldn't even have to pay for dinner since we girls were handling it and it would be really good." She pointed at Cassidy. "That was a great idea you had."

"He agreed to go to the dance with you?" Abby asked.

Devon nodded vigorously. "He certainly did."

"So you basically *asked* him?" Emma said quietly.

Devon shrugged. "What difference does it make? I'm going. Besides, that's what Bryn did."

"Not exactly," Bryn corrected. The two started arguing over it.

Emma was tempted to leave just to have some peace and quiet. Instead, she focused on eating . . . and remembering what Isaac had said to her.

"Enough," Cassidy finally said. "You guys sound like a couple of old fishwives."

"Fishwives?" Devon scowled. "Who says stuff like that anyway?"

"I do," Cassidy told her. "And it's embarrassing sitting here with you two fighting like that. Knock it off."

Emma tossed Cassidy a grateful look and continued to eat. It wasn't long until only Cassidy and Emma remained at the table.

"I don't care what Devon says," Cassidy told her. "I think it's up to you whether or not you go to the dance. If you don't feel like it, don't go."

"Thanks. I'm not sure what I'll do. But talking to Isaac did help some." Emma wiped her mouth with a napkin. "You know, he really is a very nice guy."

Cassidy patted her on the back. "Well, you deserve a nice guy, Emma."

Emma watched Cassidy as she pulled out a textbook. She appeared to be going over something for her next class, which wasn't surprising since Cassidy seemed to take her education as seriously as she took her faith. Suddenly Emma wondered why she'd so easily pushed Cass aside when Devon started attending school at Northwood. Well, except that Devon seemed to insist upon Emma's undivided devotion. Of course, Emma and Devon went so far back. Devon truly was Emma's oldest friend. Still, maybe it was a question of quality versus quantity—perhaps a *good* friend was more valuable than an *old* friend. Maybe it was something Emma should give some careful consideration.

As much as Cassidy was trying to treat her friends more kindly and respectfully, it was hard to respect Devon. Something about that girl just got under Cassidy's skin. Not only in regard to the Dating Games, although by now Cassidy felt sure that Devon's primary interest in creating the club had been purely self-serving. Beyond that, Cassidy suspected that Devon was using Emma, and sometimes it seemed that Emma didn't even notice or care. But seeing Devon treating Emma so callously today—right on the heels of Emma losing her grandfather—well, it seemed inexcusable. Yet at the same time Cassidy knew she had to forgive Devon. It was perplexing.

Cassidy was well aware that Jesus instructed his followers to love their enemies and to pray for them. She knew she couldn't use her general dislike and distrust of Devon as an excuse to blow her off or treat her badly. But as she went to jazz choir practice after school, she remembered something else Jesus had said: "Be wise as serpents but innocent as doves" (Matt. 10:16). Yes, that was how she intended to be with Devon. She'd treat Devon like a friend, but she'd be keeping an eye on her too.

Olivia Pratt stopped Cassidy as they were going into the choir room. "I hear that I have you and your friends to thank."

"What?" She studied Olivia. Was she mad about something?

"Rolf Williams asked me to go to the homecoming dance today." Olivia smiled. "He said it was because Lane had asked you and Isaac had asked Emma. Somehow you and your friends lit a fire under the guys. I don't know how you did it, but thanks."

"Uh . . . you're welcome." Cassidy wondered if anyone knew about their secret club. Probably not.

"I was so fed up with Rolf. I was about ready to say *fish or cut bait, boy.*"

"Huh?"

"You know, he was always hanging around and being friendly, but he'd never ask me out."

Cassidy glanced around. "Didn't you hear about the Worthington talk?"

Olivia waved her hand. "Everyone knows about that, but the guys don't usually take it this seriously. Anyway, it looks like the spell's been broken. I hear a lot of girls have been asked to the dance now."

"Well, that's a relief. I was afraid we might've been the only ones there." Cassidy frowned. "It makes you wonder why the school would even bother to have a dance if they really don't want us to date."

"Exactly," said another girl who'd been listening to them.

"I heard that even the faculty doesn't agree on this," Olivia confided to them. "It's no wonder the guys are dazed and confused."

The girls laughed as they took their places to start rehearsing. Cassidy felt relieved to hear others were going to the dance, but at the same time she felt uneasy too. Had the DG really undermined Worthington? And if they had, was it really something to celebrate? Fortunately, she didn't have to think about that right now. Instead she said a quick prayer and focused on singing her part.

After practice, she was on her way to the parking lot when she noticed Emma standing by herself. It looked like she was making a phone call, and it looked like she was upset. Cassidy went over just as Emma closed her phone with a frustrated expression. "What's up?" Cassidy asked her.

"Devon was supposed to give me a ride home," Emma told her. "I stayed late to help mat pictures for the art fair, and Devon was supposed to pick me up here, but as it turns out, she completely forgot." Emma looked close to tears.

"I'll give you a ride," Cassidy told her.

"Thanks." Emma sniffed. "I don't know why I had to fall apart like this."

Cassidy put a hand on her shoulder. "Hey, you just lost your grandpa. It's only natural to feel emotional, you know? It's okay."

"I guess."

"I remember when our dog died, I was a mess for weeks. And Barkley was just a dog."

Emma smiled. "Dogs can be pretty special."

Cassidy sighed to think of the sweet golden retriever she'd grown up with. "Yeah. I loved Barkley more than some of my friends." She laughed at herself. "But I'm learning to love my friends better . . . I think."

"That was cool what you said the other day," Emma said quietly. "At the DG meeting. About wanting to be a better friend and stuff. I know I didn't say much at the time, but I thought it was cool."

"Well, I took a little personal inventory." She paused to unlock her car. "I had to admit that I was lacking. I'd gotten into the habit of being so negative."

"I think it's just because you're careful," Emma said as they got into the car. "You really think about things, Cass. That's nice."

"I suppose it's good to think about things," Cassidy admitted. "But not if it makes you worried and grumpy. In that case it's better just to pray about them."

"That makes sense." Emma sighed. "My grandpa used to say something like that."

"What?"

"He said worrying was like a rocking chair—it keeps you occupied but it doesn't get you anywhere."

Cassidy chuckled as she started the car. "He was a good man, Emma. You were fortunate to have him. My favorite grandpa died when I was little. The other one lives in Florida and I never get to see him much."

"Well, at least you still have your dad."

"Yeah." Cassidy nodded. Sometimes she forgot that Emma's dad left several years ago. That had to be hard. "I guess that makes it even more important for you to have God as your Father. Really, there couldn't be a better father than God."

"My grandpa used to tell me that same thing." Emma

brightened. "You know, it's almost like God is speaking to me through my friends. It was like that with Isaac today too."

"That's very cool, Emma."

"Yeah, it's pretty comforting too." Emma sighed. "It's really good to have friends. I mean *good* friends."

"For sure." Cassidy wondered if Emma meant that some friends, like Devon, were not particularly good, but she was so not going there. Not anymore—not if she could help it. And she could.

"When is the memorial service for your grandpa?" Cassidy asked as she pulled up to Emma's house.

"Wednesday morning at the church. At 10:00."

"I'll see if I can get out of class," Cassidy told her.

"Really?" Emma sounded surprised. "You'd come?"

"Absolutely. Your grandpa was a sweet, godly man, and I'd like to honor his memory."

"Thanks." Emma gave her a sad little smile. "And thanks for the ride . . . and everything. I really, really appreciate it!"

"I'll be praying for you," Cassidy promised. "Your family too. I know it's got to be hard to lose someone you love that much. Even harder than losing Barkley." She made an apologetic smile. "Sorry, I know that doesn't even compare."

"That's okay. Sounds like Barkley was a sweet dog." Emma waved as she closed the door.

Cassidy kept her promise as she drove home. She prayed for Emma and Edward and Emma's mom and Emma's grandmother. She prayed that God would comfort all of them in a big way.

● ● ● ● ●

Cassidy attended the memorial service on Wednesday, along with Abby, Bryn, and Devon. It was a good service with a good message, but Cassidy wondered if her friends had even listened to it, because afterward it seemed that the only thing they had on their minds was their "big weekend." Or maybe that was just because Devon was monopolizing the conversation as they were leaving the church. Sometimes it was like the entire universe revolved around this self-centered girl. Did she not even care that her supposedly best friend was burying her beloved grandfather today?

"I keep assuring Jason that the dinner is going to be okay," Devon said to Cassidy as they got into Cassidy's car. She'd driven the girls to the church and was taking them back to school now. "He's still not convinced. I'm afraid he thinks it's going to be hokey."

"It won't be hokey," Bryn said defensively. "I got my aunt's recipe for this yummy Greek salad. It's to die for."

"And my dad's grilling us his special surf and turf," Cassidy told them. "Tri-tip sirloin and wild salmon."

"My mom's flourless chocolate torte is better than most restaurants'," Abby told them.

"Emma's bringing baked potatoes with everything to go with them," Cassidy told her. "Plus there'll be other things too."

"Well, you just need to do everything you can to make sure it's not a flop," Devon said in a slightly snippy tone. "I don't want Jason to be disappointed."

"Hey, he's getting a free meal," Abby declared from the backseat. "What's up with complaining about it?"

"That's right," Bryn added. "He could've been stuck shelling out a hundred bucks at the Cove. That's where most of the kids are going, and trust me, it is not cheap."

"Maybe he *wanted* to shell it out," Devon said. "And maybe I wanted to let him."

"Well, why not let him take you to the Cove?" Cassidy suggested a bit sharply. "You guys don't have to come to our little dinner." She almost pointed out that their dining table would be more comfortable with eight people anyway and that no one would miss them, but she knew that was crossing the line.

"Maybe I will," Devon said.

The car got quiet, and Cassidy wondered if she'd hurt Devon's feelings. "I mean, I'm not telling you we don't want you at our dinner," she backpedaled. "But if Jason's not into that, why not just do what you want? What's the big deal?"

"Yeah, it's not like we have DG rules about *that*," Bryn interjected.

"Although we were all going to ride to the dance together," Abby reminded them. "The guys were going in together for a limo. Jason was supposed to chip in for it."

"I'm sure he still will," Devon said. "Maybe the limo can pick us up at the restaurant. That'd be cool to come out and have it waiting there. Kinda like celebrities." She giggled. "I wonder if the paparazzi will show up."

"Yeah, right," Bryn said sarcastically.

It seemed settled. Devon and Jason would do their own thing for dinner. Since Devon had only offered to bring bread and soda for her contribution, it wouldn't be difficult to cover for her. Really, it was probably for the best. Cassidy felt certain that the four couples would have a better time without Devon and Jason there.

Hopefully Emma wouldn't be dismayed by this news. That is, if Emma had even made up her mind about going to the dance. She hadn't said anything for sure yet, but Cassidy thought she might be leaning toward going. She sure hoped she was—Emma needed something to cheer her up. And really, Isaac was good medicine. What would be the harm in going to the dance? Emma's grandpa would probably feel bad if he thought she was missing out because of him. Maybe Cassidy would tell Emma that.

Besides, she realized as she parked at school, with Devon and Jason bowing out of the dinner party, if Emma and Isaac didn't come either, that would shrink their "big" dinner party considerably. It would probably feel like a definite letdown to everyone. Especially her parents. Already they'd both gone out of their way, being so helpful with planning and preparations. Mom was acting like it was going to be such a big fancy occasion, planning for flowers and buying candles, and she'd even suggested they should polish the silver. She might be disappointed if only three couples showed.

"M"y dad is acting like a complete Neanderthal," Abby exclaimed to Bryn on the phone.

"Your sweet dad?" Bryn found this hard to believe.

"Yes. *My dad*. He says I'm not leaving the house in this—this dress." Abby's voice cracked as if she was on the verge of tears.

"What?" Bryn dropped a black satin-heeled shoe onto the floor and stood up straight. "This is so not good."

"Tell me about it."

Bryn looked at the clock by her bed. "We're supposed to be at Cass's in less than forty minutes, Abby. What're you going to do?"

"Please, please, come over," Abby pleaded. "Maybe you can help me talk some sense into the man."

"What's your mom saying?"

"I told you so."

"Huh?"

"She's saying 'I told you so' because she warned me right from the get-go that I should let Dad see the dress for approval. I know I should've shown it to him, and I was going to, but he was so busy . . . and, well, he's so overprotective of me, not to mention his taste in fashion is way too conservative." She let out a big sigh. "Yeah, I guess I thought I could sneak it beneath his radar."

"But you got caught." Bryn groaned, trying to think of a solution. "At the last minute too. What are you going to do?"

"Dad's telling me to just wear my Christmas dress from last year. Can you believe it?"

"Oh, fabulous." Bryn grabbed her shoe and shoved it on.

Abby let out a sob. "It's not even a formal, Bryn. I'll look like a total geek. Please, come over and help me. Maybe Dad will listen to you."

"Right." Bryn knew that was a long shot. Mr. Morrison was an academic man with strong opinions. Once he made up his mind about something, it was almost impossible to get him to change it.

"Please," Abby begged. "Otherwise I might as well just stay home."

"No way." Bryn was concocting a plan—or at least trying to. "Okay, I'll have Mom drop me at your house instead of Cassidy's. But your parents will have to take me to Cass's. Even if you can't go."

"I *have* to go!" she shrieked.

"I'll be there in about fifteen minutes." She shoved her other shoe on. "By the way, what is it exactly that he doesn't like about the dress?"

"He says it's *strapless*."

"But it has a strap."

"He says one strap is not enough."

"Oh." Bryn looked at her image in the mirror. Her sapphire blue dress had two straps, but they were pretty skinny. What would Mr. Morrison think about that? She could offer to trade dresses with Abby—although only for Mr. Morrison's sake, because a dress swap really wouldn't work since they were different sizes. Surely he'd think Abby's dress had more coverage than this one.

One way or another, she had to come up with a solution. As she gathered up what she needed to continue getting ready at Abby's house, she wondered if there could be a creative answer to this problem. What if they could construct something to work as another strap? She looked through her closet now, going through belts and scarves and throwing a few random pieces into her bag. Somehow she needed to remedy Abby's dress, and she needed to do it quickly. After all, she was the one who'd encouraged Abby to get the gown. Oh, bother!

She hurried downstairs, explaining to Mom that she needed to get over to Abby's ASAP. "She's having a wardrobe emergency," she told her.

"Oh dear. Poor Abby." Mom frowned. "Do you need my sewing kit?"

"Yes! Good idea." Bryn waited for Mom to return with it.

"You look beautiful." Mom kissed her cheek. "Dad said he'll drive you over. He's just getting his keys. And then we'll see you later at the Banks's."

"That's right," Bryn said. "I forgot that Mrs. Banks invited the parents for dessert."

"And for a photo shoot," Mom said. "This is so exciting."

"Yes, as long as we get Abby straightened out."

"You girls are still coming back here after the dance?" Mom asked. "For the sleepover?"

"That's the plan, Mom." Bryn reached for her bag. "All the girls dumped their stuff downstairs earlier today."

"Five hyped-up kids raising Cain down in the basement all night," Dad teased. "Reminds me of the good ol' days."

• • • • •

Before long, Bryn was in Abby's bedroom, studying the sleek purple dress and trying to think of some way—any way—to fix it. "That color is so gorgeous against your skin tone," Bryn said as she pulled various accessories out of her bag. She held up a black-and-white striped scarf, thinking it might work for dress straps, but it looked cheesy. She tried a brown suede belt, hoping it could be transformed into straps somehow, but that was all wrong too. Finally, she examined the single strap that went over Abby's shoulder and came down in the center of the dress's bodice.

"Hey, this is so wide that I'll bet I could cut it and use some of the fabric to make a second strap."

"But wouldn't it ruin the dress?" Abby frowned.

"I don't know for sure. But I do know this dress is useless if you can't go to the dance."

"Good point."

"You're certain your dad won't let you wear it as is?"

"He really put his foot down." Abby scowled. "He's convinced this dress will get me kicked out of the dance. And that would be so humiliating *for him*."

"That's ridiculous. Girls have worn dresses like this at Northwood before."

"According to my dad—he looked up the dress code on

the school's website—a dress must have at least two straps to be acceptable. He's certain that if I go like this, I'll be cast out to the streets or thrown in prison, or maybe the earth will slip off its axis."

Bryn unzipped the back of the dress. "Slip out of it and let me have a good look. I took sewing in home ec back in middle school. Let's see if I can remember anything. In the meantime, you get your hair and makeup done." She pointed at Abby's face. "I can tell you've been crying, girlfriend."

Abby sniffed. "Wouldn't you?"

"Yeah. Probably." She pulled out Mom's seam ripper and began to pick apart the seam inside the strap. She hoped this would work. After she got it apart, she pulled out the scissors. "Say a prayer," she told Abby.

"Huh?"

"For this dress." She cut into the fabric, removing a long section of fabric from underneath the strap. "Voilà." She held up the long strip. "Strap number two."

Abby frowned. "But now strap number one looks like a mess."

Bryn ignored her as she threaded a needle with black thread. "Just be patient." She proceeded to sew the strip of fabric into a narrow strap, trying to keep the stitches on the underside, which looked like a mess but hopefully would never be seen. She did the same thing to the existing strap so that now it was only about an inch wide, instead of two or more.

Abby peered over her shoulder. "Interesting. But where will you attach that other strap?"

"Put the dress on again," Bryn commanded as she re-threaded the needle with more black thread.

With Abby wearing the dress with the one now thinner

strap, Bryn played with where to put the second strap. Finally she decided to attach it in the middle so the two straps made a deep V that started in the middle, then went across *both* Abby's shoulders.

"Hey, this looks kind of cool," Bryn said after the strap was pinned into place. "Look." She spun Abby around to the mirror.

"Wow!" Abby's face broke into a huge smile. "That's even better than before. Seriously, you could be a dress designer."

Bryn grinned. "Well, I've always had a passion for fashion. Now take it off carefully, and I'll sew the second strap into place to please your sweet old daddy."

By the time Bryn had finished the dress, they had only minutes to finish getting ready. "You look fabulous," she told Abby as she reached for her makeup bag. "But I still haven't done my hair or finished my face."

"Why don't you just wear your hair down," Abby suggested as Bryn brushed on some blush, then quickly applied some mascara. "It looks beautiful."

Bryn looked at Abby's alarm clock. They should be on their way by now. "I don't think I have a choice."

"All because of me." Abby looked sad.

"Hey, it's worth it." Bryn smiled at her. "I'd go with my hair in a total mess as long as I have my best friend with me."

"I mean it, though. Your hair really does look beautiful," Abby assured her as they went downstairs.

"Let's just hope your dad doesn't put the kibosh on the dress."

"Daddy," Abby called out sweetly. "Hurry to see how Bryn fixed my dress."

Mr. Morrison emerged from his study with a book in hand,

frowning as if he expected to be disappointed. But when he saw his daughter, a slow smile crept onto his face. "See, there, Abigail. I knew you could fix it if you tried."

"Bryn fixed it," Abby informed him as she called for her mom. "Now someone needs to get us to Cassidy's so we can help get dinner set up."

"Oh, Abby," her mom said happily. "Look at you."

"It was Bryn's doing." Abby gave a little spin to show off the dress. "Isn't she brilliant?"

"Absolutely." Mrs. Morrison patted Bryn on the shoulder. "Thank you for coming to our rescue. I am hopeless with anything remotely connected to sewing."

"We gotta go, Mom," Abby urged.

"Just let me get my purse," Mrs. Morrison said. "I'm coming."

Soon they were on their way, and even though Bryn's hair was not in the sophisticated updo that she'd imagined, she was happy to sacrifice it for Abby's sake. It would've ruined everything if Abby hadn't been able to come tonight. Bryn just hoped that the dinner would go smoothly.

She knew there were only going to be four couples after Devon and Jason had bowed out—and the truth was, Bryn had been secretly relieved. It wasn't that she was jealous about Jason. Oh, maybe she'd been a little miffed at first. But after hearing more about his character—or lack of it—she felt certain she'd dodged a bullet. Whether he was great looking or not, she did not want to go out with a guy with only one thing on his mind. Devon could have him. Besides, Bryn really did like Harris, and she was looking forward to getting to know him better. Maybe he wasn't as hot as Jason, but he would probably have better manners.

Mostly she was relieved that Devon wasn't going to be at their dinner tonight. That was only because Devon had been acting like such a total brat lately. It seemed like she'd gotten bossier than ever these last few days. Ever since she'd landed a date with Jason, she'd acted like the queen bee, like she should be ruling the world. Not only did she take all the credit for the DG, but she kept acting like none of them would've gotten dates without her precious help. Really, Bryn was just about sick of it. She wouldn't miss Devon a bit tonight. Maybe when it was all said and done, she would suggest they discontinue the DG permanently. Who needed it? After the night was over, they would have experienced their first dates. It should be smooth sailing from here on out. Shouldn't it?

Devon tried not to show her disappointment when she learned Jason was not taking her to the Cove for dinner. He claimed that it was impossible to get reservations, but when they drove past the swanky restaurant, it didn't even look that busy. Instead he took her to the Alpine Inn, which was slightly run-down and smelled musty. Of course, it was not busy at all. Devon hadn't been in this restaurant since she was in grade school, but she had detested the heavy, greasy German food then, and as she skimmed the menu, she felt pretty certain she wasn't going to like it now.

"My parents always bring me here on my birthday," Jason told her as he set his menu aside. "The borscht soup is killer."

"Oh?" She nodded. Well, at least the prices were reasonable. He wouldn't have to complain about the bill. He'd already complained about the cost of renting his tux as well as the wrist corsage, which in her opinion looked like it came from the grocery store anyway. Not that *she* was complaining. He'd also bragged that he was saving money by not having to chip in for the shared limo. He had borrowed his brother's old Subaru instead, and he hadn't even bothered to wash it or clean the junk food wrappers from the backseat. Not that she was complaining. No, she was not.

She smiled across the table at him. "What do you recommend besides the borscht soup?"

"The Wiener schnitzel is my favorite. My dad likes the chicken. It's wrapped in bread dough and baked. Comes with gravy."

"Uh-huh . . ." Everything on the menu sounded fattening and boring to her. Not nearly as appealing as the dinner her friends were fixing over at Cassidy's house. Why hadn't she insisted on being there? She wondered if it was too late to change their minds. But the waitress, who looked like the Swiss Miss cocoa girl, was asking to take their order.

Devon decided on the baked chicken but passed on the borscht soup. After the waitress departed, Devon excused herself. "I need to powder my nose," she said with a forced smile.

He just laughed. "I don't know why you girls say that. Don't you think we know what you do in there?"

She faked a laugh like he was amusing, then hurried to the restroom, which was as lackluster as this restaurant, and called Emma's number. "Are you guys eating yet?" she asked Emma.

"No, we're having appetizers," Emma said cheerfully. "Abby's mom made these yummy shrimp things. To die for. Are you at the Cove?"

Devon considered lying, then wondered, why bother? "No, we're at the Alpine Inn."

"Oh?" Emma sounded concerned. "How's that going?"

"Not terribly well." Devon moved out of the way of a large elderly woman.

"Oh, my—what a pretty dress!" the woman exclaimed as she squeezed into a stall.

"Did you need something?" Emma sounded distracted on the other end. "I think it's almost time to go into the dining room." She laughed and said something to someone else. "Oh, you should see this place, Devon. I'll take some pictures. Cassidy has all these candles in jars and strings of light, and the music is perfect. Too bad you had to miss it."

"Yeah. Too bad." Devon wanted to kick something . . . or someone.

"I better go now."

"Well, I just wanted to tell you guys that you don't need to send the limo to get us. Jason has his brother's car. We'll just meet up with you at the dance. Okay?"

"Okay. Have a great dinner."

"Yeah, right." Devon turned off her phone and slid it into her evening bag. "Like that's going to happen." Still, Devon knew it was her fault that she was stuck in this cruddy little restaurant. She was the one who'd suggested that a potluck at Cass's house would be a disappointment. Jason probably would've gone for it if she'd mentioned that he could save a few bucks as well as be with friends. However, she'd imagined them dining alone in sophistication, not squalor.

It was unfair to blame him. And besides, she reminded herself, Jason was one of the hottest guys in school. Wasn't that worth something? So what if his manners lacked a little polish. Or even if his taste in restaurants was pathetic. He was easy to look at. At the very least she could brag to others that she had dined alone with him this evening. Really, did the rest of it matter so much?

"Get over yourself," she said as she emerged from the restroom. "Have some fun."

• • • • •

"Everything was so delicious," Lane said to the group sitting around the table. They'd finished with the dinner and were about to start on dessert. "You girls could open a restaurant if you wanted to."

"Not without our parents' help," Cassidy reminded him. "My dad was the main chef tonight. But Bryn made the salad and Emma did the potatoes."

"I *helped* make the dessert," Abby announced as she set a piece of chocolate torte à la mode in front of him. "But if you guys like it, I'll take the full credit."

"This has been so much fun already," Bryn said happily. "And we still have the dance to look forward to."

"I'm glad I decided to do this," Kent told Abby as she set a piece of cake in front of him.

"Decided?" Harris teased him. "Don't you mean we let the girls bully us into it?"

"Bully you?" Bryn pretended to be hurt. "Really? Is that how you feel?"

"Hey, we just needed some encouragement," Isaac said to Emma.

"And that's exactly what we gave you," Emma told him.

"Here's to encouragement." Bryn held up her water glass for a toast.

"To encouragement," they all echoed.

"Devon called earlier," Emma said. "I think she was wishing she was here."

"Why didn't they come?" Kent asked.

"I'm not sure," Emma said. She was still feeling sorry for Devon and wondering why Jason would've picked that restaurant to eat at.

"Because Jason wanted to spend money to impress her," Bryn said in a teasing tone. "At least that's what Devon thought."

"That doesn't sound like the Jason I know," Harris said.

Lane nodded. "Yeah. Jason is usually kind of a cheapskate."

"Then why didn't he want to come here?" Cassidy asked. "The price was certainly right."

The guys exchanged knowing looks but didn't say anything.

"Well, it doesn't matter," Bryn said. "We're having a good time, and we'll catch up with them later anyway."

Emma still felt slightly worried for Devon's sake. The more she learned about Jason, the less she liked him. Even so, she hoped that Devon wouldn't be too disappointed over tonight. Especially after Devon's work on getting the DG together. Really, based on how it was going at Cassidy's house, the DG had been a success.

The parents had already arrived armed with cameras, so shortly after dessert was finished, the four couples took turns posing. After about twenty minutes, the limo arrived and gave them the perfect excuse to make an exit.

"You girls are still having that sleepover at Bryn's house after the dance, *right*?" Abby's overly protective dad called this out loudly enough for everyone to hear. Almost as if he didn't trust his daughter. Or maybe it was the boys he didn't trust. For a split second, Emma was glad her father wasn't around to embarrass her like that. Then again, maybe it would be nice.

"I feel like a celebrity," Bryn said as they got into the back of the stretch limo. "This is too fun."

"Too bad Devon is missing out," Emma said wistfully.

"Hey, it was her choice," Abby reminded her.

They continued to laugh and joke, enjoying themselves all the way to the school, where the dance was being held in the gymnasium. Although the gym was decorated, the girls agreed as they gathered in the bathroom that it felt anticlimactic after their lovely dinner.

Still, they had fun dancing and being together. Eventually Devon and Jason showed up. Emma could tell that Devon was trying to put on a game face so that the rest of the group wouldn't guess how unhappy she really was, but Emma had known Devon for years. She knew that Devon wasn't just unhappy, she was mad.

"Come to the restroom with me," she said as she grabbed Emma by the hand. "I need a girlfriend."

"Sure." Emma waved at Isaac. "I'll be back in a few," she called.

"I am so mad," Devon hissed as she ushered Emma toward the restroom. "I have to let off some steam before I explode all over everyone."

"I'm sorry," Emma said. "Was dinner really bad?"

"Don't even get me going."

Emma was about to say how great their dinner was but stopped herself. That would not help. "Well, you're here now," Emma said positively. "Maybe it'll get better."

"Yeah." Devon touched up her lip gloss. "I don't think it could get worse." She lowered her voice. "Jason is, shall we say, very frugal."

"Hey, frugal is good," Emma told her. "I'm frugal too."

Devon rolled her eyes. "I mean he's cheap, Emma. Stingy. You should've seen the miserly tip he left. Sure, the waitress was awful, but it was still embarrassing."

Emma put a consoling hand on Devon's shoulder. "Put it behind you," she said soothingly. "Just have fun. Everyone else is. And we could say it's because of you, Devon. You were the one who thought of the DG." She smiled. "And it worked."

Devon's stressed expression relaxed a little. "Yeah, it did, didn't it?"

Emma nodded eagerly. "All thanks to you."

Devon actually smiled now.

"Let's go have fun," Emma said cheerfully.

"Yes!" Devon said with enthusiasm. "Let's!"

For the rest of the evening, Devon was back to her usual happy-go-lucky self. She seemed as if she'd completely forgotten her lousy dinner date, and Emma felt like having Devon and Jason around made it more fun and lively for everyone. As the evening was coming to an end, Jason and Devon announced that they were getting ready to leave.

"Last ones to arrive and first ones to leave," Bryn observed.

"You guys think you're too good for us?" Abby teased.

"Maybe we just need some alone time," Jason told them with a twinkle in his eyes.

"I'll catch up with you girls at Bryn's house," Devon told them. "Don't wait up for me." She laughed.

"What's that supposed to mean?" Emma asked no one in particular.

"Who knows?" Cassidy just shook her head.

Emma tried not to obsess over Devon, but she couldn't help but feel concerned. What if Devon was in over her head with Jason? What if what Bryn had overheard Amanda saying in the restroom was true? Emma had seen that gleam in his eye. He seemed awfully eager to get Devon alone. And he'd already boasted to everyone that he didn't take the Worthington speech seriously.

What if Jason didn't behave like a gentleman tonight? Still, Emma assured herself, if anyone could handle a boy like that, it would be Devon. Good grief. Devon had gone to one of the roughest public high schools in the city. She'd been around all sorts of boys—and liked to brag about it to Emma sometimes. Really, with the dance about to end, it was a waste of time for Emma to fret and worry about Devon. Devon could take care of herself!

After the dance, the guys insisted on taking the girls out for ice cream. Naturally their formal attire garnered plenty of looks from the other customers. "Are you movie stars?" a young girl with wide eyes asked Abby as they were leaving.

Abby laughed. "I guess it's kind of like we're starring in our own movie," she told the girl. "But we're not really famous."

They made it to Bryn's house just before midnight—the curfew that Abby's dad had embarrassingly insisted upon with all parents present. Abby knew her dad loved her. She just sometimes wished he could tone it down a little.

The guys, still acting in a gentlemanly fashion, got out of the limo and escorted their dates onto the front porch to say good night. Suddenly Abby felt nervous—what if Kent wanted to kiss her? She just wasn't ready for that. She tried not to spy on her friends, scattered about in the shadows of the porch, although she was curious as to how they were handling it.

"Thanks for a great evening," Kent said politely as he reached for her hand.

"Thank you," she told him, relieved that he was simply shaking her hand. "I really had fun."

"It's been great getting to know you better," he said a bit shyly. "Maybe dating's not so bad, huh?"

She fiddled with her wilting wrist corsage. "Yeah, maybe not."

Then, just like that, the good-nights were finished and the guys returned to the limo. The girls went into the house, where they immediately burst into nervous giggles.

"Well, that was awkward," Bryn said as they tromped down to the family room in the basement. "Four couples on the same porch saying good night at the same time."

"I happened to like it," Abby told her as she kicked off her shoes. "It felt like there was safety in numbers."

"Yeah, I guess so . . . if you want to be safe." Bryn had a sly expression.

"Ooh," Emma teased. "Sounds like someone wanted to be kissed."

Bryn shrugged as she began peeling off her gown. "Maybe . . ."

As the girls got out of their dresses and into more comfortable clothes, they continued talking about the evening and what they'd liked or not liked about their first date.

"Maybe we should be putting this in the DG notebook," Cassidy said suddenly.

"Yeah," Emma agreed. "Especially since Devon is missing out."

"Who knows," Bryn added. "We might want it for future reference."

Emma went over to Devon's things and dug around until she found the DG notebook, then handed it to Cassidy. "Here, since you're secretary."

"I have an idea." Cassidy opened the book. "How about if we rate our dates?"

"Rate our dates?" Abby made herself comfortable in a corner of the big sectional. "Interesting."

"We'll have categories," Cassidy continued as she wrote. "Like for things like promptness and politeness."

"Appearance too." Bryn opened a bag of chips and set it on the coffee table. "There's soda in the fridge."

"How about a category for treating us with respect," Emma added.

"And one for just plain fun," Abby suggested.

"Okay, here's what I have so far." Cassidy read from the notebook:

1. Promptness
2. Politeness
3. Respectfulness
4. Appearance
5. Fun

"I think that's plenty," Abby said. "We don't want to over-complicate it."

"How about if we give them stars?" Bryn suggested. "Five stars is tops—as good as it gets. One star is so-so." Using the guys' code names, they started to rank their dates. For the most part the guys were receiving four to five stars.

"But we have to give Kent and Lane just two stars on promptness since they were late for dinner," Abby said.

"That's because they took extra time getting ready," Bryn

interjected, "and for that they should both get five stars for appearance—because they looked hot." On and on they went, arguing sometimes and changing the stars occasionally, until they'd rated all four boys.

"Not bad." Cassidy held up the book. "On average, it looks like we had pretty good dates. Impressive for our first dates."

"Yeah, but there's still room for improvement," Abby said.

"We haven't gotten Devon's report yet," Cassidy pointed out.

"I wonder what's keeping her." Emma looked worried. "It's almost 1:00 now."

The room got quiet, and then Bryn wrinkled her nose. "Jason probably took her up to Arden Butte to 'look at the stars.'" She laughed. Of course, they all knew why couples *really* went to Arden Butte.

"I hope she's okay," Emma said quietly.

"Of course she's okay," Bryn assured her. "Devon's one tough cookie. If anyone could keep Jason in line, it's her."

Abby wondered if Devon would even want to keep Jason in line. So often Devon gave the impression that she wanted to have a wild time. Well, maybe she was having one tonight.

"You guys ready for the movie?" Bryn asked as she held up a DVD. "I got *50 First Dates*. I thought it sounded apropos."

The others laughed. Just as she slid it into the player, someone's cell phone rang. "Who's calling this late?" Cassidy asked.

"Maybe the guys are missing us already," Bryn joked.

"I think it's me." Emma scrambled for her bag. Fumbling, she answered. Everyone got quiet, and it was obvious she was talking to Devon. "Where are you?" Emma said urgently. "Are you okay?" She listened. "Wait a second, let me ask."

She held the phone down and looked at the others. "Does anyone have a car? So we can go get her?"

"Go get her?" Bryn frowned. "Why doesn't Jason just bring her here?"

"Because Jason deserted her over by Henson Reservoir," Emma whispered.

"Henson Reservoir?" Abby was shocked. "What were they doing over there?"

"What do you think?" Bryn said in a slightly snarky tone.

"She sounds hysterical," Emma hissed. "We've got to help her."

"I've got my car here," Cassidy said quickly. "I can go get her. Find out where she is exactly. I'm guessing it'll take us about fifteen or twenty minutes."

Emma asked and then promised they were on their way. "But stay on the phone," she insisted. "We'll keep talking to you until we get there."

"Just like 911," Bryn said in a teasing tone.

"Be nice," Abby told her. "It sounds like Devon really needs us."

Bryn nodded. "Sorry."

"Let's go," Cassidy said. "I mean, whoever wants to—not everyone has to come." They all insisted on coming anyway.

"Do you need to tell your parents?" Abby asked Bryn.

Bryn just shrugged. "Wake them up?"

Abby knew that if this was her house, her dad would expect to be informed. However, it was not. She would leave it up to Bryn.

"Let's be quiet," Bryn said as she led the way up the stairs. "No sense in waking everyone."

Soon they were in Cassidy's car and on their way to the

lake. Emma continued to keep Devon on the line, but it sounded like Emma was doing all the talking, rambling on and on about their dates and the dance and even about how they'd made a rating system for the guys.

Finally, Cassidy turned into a picnicking area, and there waving her arms at them was Devon. In the headlights, they could see that Devon's hair was messed up. Her gown looked rumpled and dirty, and one of the straps was torn.

"Looks like she's had a rough time," Bryn said quietly as Emma leaped out of the car and ran to her. The others got out too and huddled protectively around Devon. She burst into loud sobbing.

"It's going to be okay," Emma said soothingly as they guided her back to the car. Emma, Devon, and Abby got into the backseat, with Devon in the middle.

Abby handed Devon her bottle of water. "Here, maybe this will help."

"What happened?" Bryn asked from the front. "Should we take you to the police station?"

"The police station?" Abby was shocked and then scared—what would her dad say about this? "What for?"

Bryn turned around, giving Abby a serious look. "Haven't you ever heard of date rape?"

Abby cringed. "Is that what happened, Devon?"

Devon made a growling sound. "No," she said sharply. "He did *not* rape me."

Emma sighed. "Oh, that's a relief."

"But you look so messed up," Abby said. "Like you were in a fight or an accident or something."

"It was a fight," Devon conceded.

"With Jason?" Emma asked.

"Yes." Devon took a drink of the water.

"Why did you come way out here?" Cassidy asked as she drove toward town.

"Jason wanted to come out here to see the moon on the lake. I'll admit that sounded romantic and exciting and fun—at first. But then all he wanted to do was make out, and, well, you know how that can go." She sniffed, using the back of her hand to wipe her nose. "Anyway, he started getting pretty pushy. Naturally, I pushed back. He acted like it was a game then. And he acted like I owed him something."

"Just like what I overheard from Amanda," Bryn said.

"I guess." Devon took in a deep breath. "He wouldn't take no for an answer. Finally I just let him have it."

"Let him have it?" Abby asked.

"I kicked him," Devon told her. "Right where it hurts. You know?"

Abby nodded slowly. "Oh . . . yeah."

"Well, I got him good," Devon said. "He was so mad he started swinging at me, but he was in so much pain, it was pretty pointless. Then he walked off and I thought he was just going to cool off, but he got in the car and drove away." She started crying again. "He just dumped me out here in the middle of nowhere. Can you believe it?"

"Hey, that's better than what might've happened," Bryn said.

"At least you had your phone," Abby pointed out.

"And your friends," Emma added.

Devon was crying hard again, so Abby and Emma wrapped their arms around her, both of them promising that she'd feel better when they got home. "Bryn has a fun movie for us to watch," Emma said softly. "And junk food."

Devon took in a jagged breath. "You guys are really the best," she said in a choked voice. "I don't know what I'd have done without you tonight."

"Hey, that's what friends are for," Abby said gently. Although she felt bad for Devon's sake since she'd had such a lousy evening, part of Abby was grateful. Somehow coming out here like this in the middle of the night and rescuing Devon had brought them all closer. This whole night had been kind of a bonding experience for them. She realized that if they hadn't created the DG, none of this would've happened.

Bryn was the one who called a meeting of the DG on Monday. "Five o'clock at Costello's," she informed her friends. Cassidy suspected the reason for the meeting was because some of the girls seemed ready to disband their little club. Perhaps that was a good thing. After all, hadn't Cassidy been opposed to this idea in the beginning? Of the five girls, she'd been the heel-dragger. But for some reason, she felt differently now.

As usual, thanks to jazz choir practice, she was the last one to join them at Costello's. Bryn had already ordered her a coffee. "Thanks," she said as she took the empty chair. "Sorry to be late again. The concert is this week, so no more after-school practices after Wednesday."

"Well, as you know, I wanted us to meet," Bryn began. "Now that we've all had our first dates, and now that the guys have been freed from Worthington's spell."

"It's not a spell," Emma said defensively. "According to

Isaac, it's just a commitment to be honorable toward girls. If you ask me, that's a good thing."

"Yeah, yeah." Bryn nodded. "I know—I know. Anyway, my point is, now that we've sort of broken the ice, you know, in the whole dating arena . . . well, I just wonder how necessary it is to keep our little club going."

"Meaning you don't need anyone's help getting dates from now on?" Abby said to her.

Bryn shrugged. "I'm not saying that. I just wonder if the DG has outgrown its usefulness."

"You're saying the only purpose of the DG was to get us dates?" Emma asked pointedly.

"Well, wasn't it?" Bryn frowned.

"Maybe . . ." Emma looked hurt now. "I guess I thought we were friends too."

"Well, of course we're friends," Bryn told her. "That hasn't changed."

"To be fair," Abby jumped in, "Devon started this club as a way to get the guys to start dating. Right, Devon?"

Devon, who had been very quiet all day, just nodded. Her expression was somber.

"So what do you think about it?" Bryn asked Devon. "Do you want the club to end?"

Devon's expression was hard to read, but Cassidy thought she was upset. Maybe she was still stewing over her bad date with Jason. "The club belongs to all of us," Cassidy said quietly. "If we're considering ending it, I think it should be put to a vote."

"Fine," Bryn said. "Let's vote."

"Not yet," Cassidy told her. "First, I'd like to open it up for discussion."

"Isn't that what we were doing?" Bryn demanded.

"Well, we've heard your opinion," Cassidy told her. "But not everyone has spoken up."

Bryn nodded. "Okay, does anyone else have anything to say?"

"I do." Abby held up her hand, then, looking sheepishly around the table, she put it down. "I want to say that I kind of like the DG. I feel like I learned a lot about dating and boys and stuff. But the best part of it was getting to know you guys better. I'm not sure I want that to end. To be honest, I feel like I'm still figuring out this whole dating thing too. I had fun on my date with Kent, but I honestly don't think I'm ready to go out on a date with just me and a guy. That makes me really nervous. It would make my dad nervous too. So I'm not so sure I want to part with the DG. Not just yet, anyway."

"Oh." Bryn looked surprised. "I didn't know that."

"You never asked me," Abby told her.

"I understand how Abby feels," Emma added. "I'm not very secure around boys either. Not like some of you—like Bryn and Devon—"

"Don't include me on that list," Devon said hotly.

"Well, you always act like you know all about boys," Emma told her. "Like you're the expert."

"Well, I'm not. Okay?" Devon glared at her. "I'm sorry if I gave you that impression. I would think that after seeing what happened to me on Saturday you would get that, Emma."

Emma blinked. "Fine. I get it. Sorry."

Devon softened now. "Sorry . . . I didn't mean to go ballistic on you. I guess I'm feeling a little sensitive. Especially when it comes to boys. I am not the expert. Okay?"

Emma held her hands up. "Okay, okay. I get that."

"Good." Devon pointed at Bryn. "I guess you're the expert now."

"*Moi?*" Bryn shook her head. "I don't think so."

"Come on," Cassidy jumped in. "Let's agree that none of us is an expert when it comes to boys or dating. Okay?"

They all nodded and agreed.

"Like we said early on, maybe there is safety in numbers," she continued.

"You can say that again," Devon concurred.

"And the Dating Games are like other games," Cassidy reminded them. "We learn as we play and go along. There's nothing wrong with that."

"We've got a good set of rules," Emma pointed out.

"So maybe we shouldn't be so quick to give up on this," Abby said.

"Are we ready to put it to a vote?" Bryn asked.

"One more thing." Cassidy looked around the table. "I want to go on the record as saying that I think the most important thing about this club isn't learning about dating and boys."

"What are you saying?" Bryn asked.

"Well, I know some of you have hinted at this too," Cassidy continued. "I think the most important part of the DG—and it's the reason I want this club to continue—is our friendships. The DG has taught me more about being a good friend than it has about dating. Quite honestly, I don't want to venture into the dating world without some trustworthy girlfriends backing me up. We need each other. I have a feeling it could be rough out there."

"That's for sure," Devon said. "I can attest to that."

"Now are we ready to put it to a vote?" Bryn asked. "All

in favor of keeping the Dating Games club going for a while, raise your hand." All the hands went up, and the girls burst into laughter. "I guess we're stuck with each other," Bryn said happily. "The truth is, I didn't really want the club to end, but I just assumed everyone else would."

"I need this club," Devon told them in a serious tone. "I need you guys for my friends too. I'm sorry if I gave the wrong impression a while back. I know I can come across as snotty and arrogant sometimes—usually when I'm feeling insecure. I'll try to do better."

They talked a while longer, and it was obvious that everyone was hugely relieved that the DG had not been abolished. Perhaps none more so than Cassidy, which was ironic when she considered how opposed she'd been back in the beginning. However, it seemed quite clear that they all needed each other.

"So," Cassidy said slowly as they were getting ready to leave. "I have a little news flash for everyone."

"What is it?" Bryn asked.

"The reason I wasn't in the cafeteria today at lunchtime was because I went to an Honor Society meeting."

"Because you're, like, the brainiac of the group?" Devon said teasingly but with a smile.

"No, that's not why I told you that," Cassidy clarified. "The topic of discussion at the meeting was our fall fundraiser. Honor Society is going to host a masquerade ball on Halloween, and, well, I wondered if the DG would like to start planning for our next dates."

"Yes!" Bryn said with enthusiasm.

"But do we have to have the same dates as last time?" Abby asked. "I mean, I like Kent and all, but I'm not sure I want to go out with him again. It's not like we're a couple."

"I know I do *not* want to go out with Jason—ever again!" Devon declared.

"I'm open to going out with someone else," Cassidy agreed. "Lane is nice, but I don't want to get serious."

"I have an idea," Devon said suddenly. "How about *blind* dates?"

"Blind dates?" Bryn looked horrified.

Devon chuckled. "Yes, guys like Darrell Zuckerman, you know?"

Bryn looked even more worried. "Seriously?"

"Hey, it could be fun," Cassidy told her. "We'd really have to trust each other, wouldn't we?"

"And since it's a masquerade thing, we'd be in costumes, so you wouldn't even have to know who you were with," Emma added.

"Are you guys in?" Devon asked with enthusiasm. "I mean, doesn't it sound like fun?"

"Let's vote," Bryn suggested. After some more discussion, they put it to a vote—and it was unanimous.

"There we have it," Cassidy declared as she wrote it in the notebook. "The next big date for the DG will be blind dates—for the masquerade ball on Halloween. Sounds like fun!"

Melody Carlson is the award-winning author of over two hundred books, including *The Jerk Magnet*, *The Best Friend*, *The Prom Queen*, *A Simple Song*, and the Diary of a Teenage Girl series. Melody recently received a Romantic Times Career Achievement Award in the inspirational market for her books. She and her husband live in central Oregon. For more information about Melody, visit her website at www.melodycarlson.com.

Meet Melody at
MelodyCarlson.com

· ·

- Enter a contest for a signed book
- Read her monthly newsletter
- Find a special page for book clubs
- Discover more books by Melody

Become a fan on Facebook
Melody Carlson Books

Stories of Young Love, Friendship, and
BEING YOURSELF

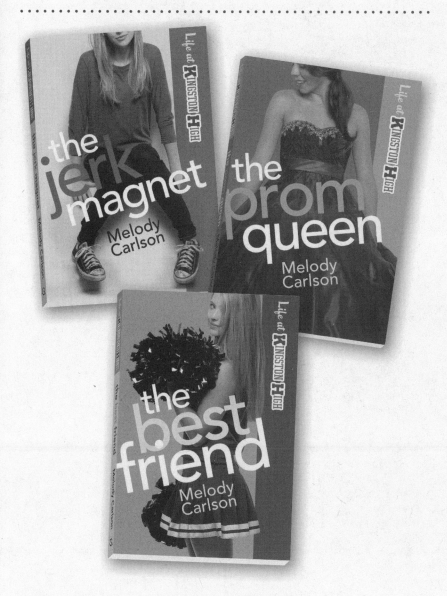

"Carlson hits all the right notes in this wonderful story that grips you from the beginning and does not let go."
—*RT Reviews*, **TOP PICK!**

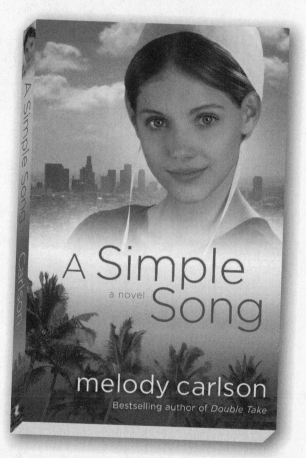

Katrina Yoder has the voice of an angel, but her Amish parents believe singing is prideful vanity. When she wins a ticket to sing in Hollywood, her life is turned upside down.

God is speaking.
ARE YOU LISTENING?

Melody unpacks and applies his words to all of your life—school, family, relationships, and more. *Devotions for Real Life* gives you words you can depend on through all the ups and downs and runarounds of your world.